> **"This dumb town, as we know, can be a very tricky place."**
>
> —Tara Maureen Murphy

It's 1991, and **Tara Maureen Murphy** is finally on top. A frightening cross between Regina George and Tracy Flick, Tara is any high school's worst nightmare: ambitious, narcissistic, manipulative, and jealous. She's got a hot jock boyfriend and a loyal best friend, and she's poised to star as Sandy in South High's production of *Grease*. Clinching the role is just one teensy step in Tara's plot to get out of her hometown and become the Broadway starlet she was born to be.

The arrival of freshman **Matthew Bloom**, however, and his dazzling audition for the role of Danny Zuko, turns Tara's world upside down. Freshmen belong in the chorus, not the spotlight! But Tara's outrage is tinged with an unfamiliar emotion, at least to her: adoration. What starts as a conniving ploy to "mentor" young Matt quickly turns into a romantic obsession that threatens to topple Tara's hard-won status at South High. . . .

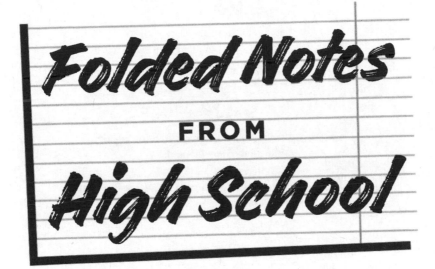

Folded Notes FROM High School

a novel

MATT BOREN

RAZORBILL®

RAZORBILL®

An Imprint of Penguin Random House LLC

Penguin.com

RAZORBILL & colophon is a registered trademark
of Penguin Random House LLC.

First published in the United States of America by Razorbill, an imprint of
Penguin Random House LLC, 2018

LIBRARY OF CONGRESS CATALOGING-IN-PUBLICATION DATA IS AVAILABLE

ISBN: 9780451478207

Printed in the United States of America

1 3 5 7 9 10 8 6 4 2

Book design by Corina Lupp

For my parents, Daryl and Joe,

who gave me a pen that's never run out of ink.

The FOLDED NOTE (*n.*) was a popular form of communication in high schools across America in the 1980s and 1990s, providing a forum for friends and lovers alike to share their most intimate thoughts about the world, their teenage angst, and the twists and turns in their hearts. Written on college-ruled notebook paper, notes were often folded and passed in high school hallways, shoved into book bags, pocketbooks, lockers, and desks. Folded notes were often sprayed with perfume or cologne and decorated with hearts, stars, and other doodles to enhance the reading experience. In the late 1980s, folded notes grew in size, becoming more than handwritten sound bites, but shared diary entries, short stories, or monologues. As the folded notes expanded, new folding techniques emerged to address the fact that notes were getting too thick to sneak into locker vents. No one is certain who invented the great flattening technique whereby one takes one's thick folded note and presses it in the center of a math textbook, but that concept alone allowed for folded notes to get bigger and bigger, all the while enabling teenagers to continue passing them discreetly through the hallways of high schools across America.

The following account represents the folded note correspondence surrounding one Tara Maureen Murphy, senior at South High School, c. 1991–92.

SEPTEMBER 1991

Dearest Christopher,

What's up? Q even believe we are 1 day away from being Seniors? Who woulda thought that I, Tara Maureen Murphy, and you, Christopher Patrick Caparelli, would end up a Supercouple after all this time? I guess what people say is wicked true, C.P.C.—summer before Senior year is super important slash life-changin'.

Christopher, you're the best thing that ever happened to me in this two-bit town. I've been longing to get the hell outta this place, but now that I'm with you . . . well, it doesn't seem so bad here after all. Suddenly, Shoppers World seems like a magical kingdom and not some average outdoor mall. Don't get me wrong, Christopher. I AM NOT A TOWNIE! I long to see the world. A girl's gotta make moves, know what I mean? But for now, my heart is here. With you. If you don't dance with me when they play "I've Had the Time of My Life" at Prom, I am gonna be devastated. 'Cuz the song says it all, Mr. Mister . . . I HAVE had the time of my life, and you wanna know who I owe it all to, Christopher? You! Durr!

God, I shoulda listened to Kim McCardle all those years ago when she swore hockey players are the sexiest. Ohhhhh, Christopher. J'teme (that's French, silly). No matter where I go to University (better be NYU!!) I will be "Forever Your Girl" (ATTENTION: Paula Abdul, if you're reading this note . . . stop reading . . . THIS is a PRIVATE NOTE. J TO THE K) (that means "just kidding").

K . . . I gotta run now. Goin' shopping so I can get an awesome top to go with my candy cane miniskirt. A girl's gotta look hot on the first day of school. I cannot wait to meet my guy under the stairwell in F Hall so we can make out as dumb teachers walk by.

Forever and a day,
Tara Maureen Murphy

P.S. I have auditions for the Fall Musical at the end of the week, so don't bother me!! If I don't get to play Sandy I will go crazy!

P.P.S. I will totally be nice to your neighbor slash freshman friend, Adam. Or is it Marty? Wait, I feel so stupid because I simply can't remember . . . what is his name? Oh yeah . . . Matt.

Dear Tara,

Sweet. A note in my mailbox. Awesome way to start Senior year. I'm gonna swing by your house on the way to finally gettin' a sunroof cut into my car, and I'm gonna stick this in your mailbox.

I will dance the crap outta you at Prom. Don't even worry. When that song comes on, I will be dirty dancing all over your face. And I know it's wicked far in advance, but we should rent a stretch from Kurt Cutter's dad's company and definitely go with Tzoug and whoever he is dating, Dube and whoever he is dating, and obviously Stef and whoever she's hooking up with—I mean dating. Hey, maybe we can finally get her interested in Tzoug or Dube. How awesome would life be if there could be another couple in town as sick as us, especially if one is my best friend and one is your best friend? Sick, right? So friggin' psyched for Senior year!

Oh and yeah, my across-the-street neighbor's name is Matt. Matt Bloom. You can call him Matty B. He's into all that theater stuff, too. If you see him in the hallways or at auditions, just say hi to the little guy. I'm sure the hottest girl in school saying hi to him would make him feel pretty cool.

I gotta go to the gym. These muscles don't just happen. Wish you had let me buy you that claddagh ring so everyone could know you were mine, but hey . . . maybe down the line? I also wish I was under the F Hall stairs with you right now!! But hey . . . we got all year, and I've got that old giant-sized vodka bottle from my dad and it's filled with pennies, so I'm not concerned about wishes.

See you tomorrow morning. First day of Senior year. I can't wait to see that candy cane skirt.

Love ya,

C.P.C.

To-est Soup!

Hi, other most beautiful girl in New England! And so it is, we have officially been goin' to school together since kindergarten—that's 13 years, Tomato!

Okay, first of all, could you look more gorgeous on the first day of our Senior year? I'll answer that! NO! Oh my god, what did your mom (my second mom, and let's be real, my first mom on most days) feed you in Nantucket all summer? Gorgeous pills?! We should dress identical this week and walk down the halls in slow motion—the school will literally freak out.

I missed you more than life this summer. Not havin' my best friend around for TWO MONTHS really shined a light on what it's gonna be like when we go to college. We've been together, like, every day our whole lives. (Except this past summer, Miss Nantucket (tee-hee, tee-hee), so happy for you that your family got a cottage there!) Were you sooo lonely there without me? I'm sure it's beautiful, and you had your family, but NO BEST FRIEND FOR THAT LONG! Well, what am I even saying, I know how you felt because from our friendship pins to our matching telephone-wire bracelets to our best friends necklace . . . I know everything you feel because I feel it, too. And I was lonely without you. Don't get me wrong, I had Christopher, but nothing replaces my Stefanie, Stef, Steffed-Animal, Soup!

So, now that you're a supermodel, who do you wanna go out with? Tara and Christopher, Stef and blank? We have to be very, veeery careful about who your boyfriend will be. No one is good enough for you (we know that), but let's make a list.

While you were in Nantucket this summer I changed my entire bedroom. You are gonna freak, it's so good! You know my little corkboard to the side of my desk that I had all our movie stubs (*Mystic Pizza*, *Pump Up the Volume*, etc., etc.) and concert tickets (NKOTB, Paula Abdul, etc., etc.) on? Gone! I was like, "Tara, you do not need two corkboards as a Senior, and Tara, you do not need to have all your memories with your best friend EVER out for any not-as-important person to see, because my lifetime history with Stef Campbell is no one's business except for me, Stef, and my diaries . . . duh." So, yes . . . I now have a one-corkboard bedroom. Classier, college-ish, right?

I got brand-new sheets at TJ's! I know you're like, "Wait, you got rid of your hearts-and-stars sheets? You lived for those!" I know, Stef . . . Q even believe? But I'm growin' up and so is my bed. Oh, my new sheets are just white. Off-white kind of, but I wanted a clean slate. It's not every day you start your final year of high school!

I feel like you were in Nantucket ALL summer! Well, I guess that's 'cuz you were. Do islands like that not have phones (tee-hee, tee-hee)—no, but for real (not for fake), I missed hearin' your voice, Minnie Strone! Tell me everything about your time there. Were you so bored with no best friend? Wait, did I already ask you that? Well, I hope you carried me with you all summer, and I'm sure you held your half of the necklace as much as I held mine (every day!).

Christopher and I are already talkin' about Prom. You are coming with us no matter who you are dating (we need to make that list ASAP). Do you think Tzoug or Dube is cute for you? Whatever. You know Christopher, he is like dyin' for there to be another Supercouple in this town like me and him.

Anyway, I am beyond hopeful that I get cast as Sandy in *Grease*. You think I will, right? Of course you do, you're like, "Tara, YOU ARE SANDY!" I know, I know. I gotta stay calm, just wicked excited to play her.

I wonder what Senior Superlatives we're gonna get come spring! Can we split Most Beautiful (like our necklace)??

OH MY GOD, WE ARE SENIORS!!!

Okay, I love you "More Than Words."

Your best friend (and don't you forget it),

Lives, Loves, Laughs (TRIPLE *L* for LIFE!),
Tar

P.S. Christopher's across-the-street neighbor is a Freshman and apparently interested in theater. Think I should write him a welcome note?

To-est Tara, T. Murphs, Tmurphette,

I can't wait to see your "new" room! It sounds fabulous. And yes, you were so right, I was like, "Holy crap, Tara got rid of her hearts-and-stars sheets!" My god, the memories. Those sheets have been with us 4-eva! They're, like, famous. If you didn't throw them out maybe we can cut them up and sew them into something else.

I know, I sew now. Such a long story, but it's you, so I have to tell you.

When we first got to Nantucket I was crying all the time. And I felt terrible about it because this cottage has been my parents' dream for, like, their whole lives, and here I was bawling my eyes out because I was away from home, away from you. And, yes, Nantucket does have phones and we do have one at our cottage but my parents' only rule was for all of us to "stay present, be off the grid." Easier said than done! I mean, that first week there was so intense, Tara! Like I couldn't even see how beautiful the island was, and oh my god, it is so beautiful. You have to come to the cottage with me one day. Pinky swear you will?

So, it was the Fourth of July, which is a bigger deal on Nantucket than even those times we went to the Hatch Shell. People take the 4th wicked seriously on island. And so my family biked into town for the festivities. We did a sandwich grab at Something Natural—the greatest sandwiches in the world— and then we were off to the boats. Most of the roads there are cobblestone, so biking at first was wicked challenging, but when you get the hang of it it's awesome!

And you know me when I'm sad. Well, you totally do because you used to be the only person on the planet who could make me NOT SAD!

So I'm, like, feeling super lonely on island and it's the 4th, which I always spend with you, and then I ran into, literally, Stacey Simon! My sandwich flew out of my bike basket, and I flew into a tree, and my bike landed on top of Stacey!

All I could think to myself was, "I hate Nantucket. Of all the people in the world to run over, it had to be the biggest bitch in our entire school!"

I was dying. My whole family stopped and peeled me off the tree, and then we all went over to help Stacey. Her knees were wicked cut up, and I thought she was gonna kill me. But she didn't. I was like, "I am SO SORRY!" And the first thing she said was, "Stef Campbell?" I was like, "Umm, yeah." And she was like, "I didn't know you come to Nantucket." And I told her it was our first summer there, and she told me her family has had a house there since '85, which I knew, obviously, because everyone in our town knows everything about Stacey Simon, right? But I played dumb, and I was like, "You have a house here, too? Wow!" And my family helped her up, and we were all apologizing so much, and I offered my T-shirt to her so she could stop her bleeding—I had my bathing suit under it—and she was like, "Oh my god, no, it's okay." And she took the bandana out of her hair and used that to, like, stop her knees from bleeding out.

Anyway, she invited me over to her house, which was totally surreal. I thought she hated us! But I was like, "I'm on island. I don't know anyone here. Sure." So, I biked over, like, the next day. Oh my god, their house is on the ocean, and it is so incredible! And she has a sewing machine in her bedroom there, and she collects all these great Nantucket fabrics and makes her own blankets. I was like, "Stacey Simon sews?!" And she taught me. So now I sew.

I can teach you! We should for sure make something out of your old hearts-and-stars sheets . . . if you didn't throw them out.

I am so excited for this year, Tar! Let's definitely make a plan to hang out and make a list of who I might date. Hmmm . . . so many possibilities, right?

And who else could play Sandy in *Grease*? NO ONE! You truly are SANDY!

Triple *L* for Life!

Love you Muchly and Moreso,
Soup

Oh, and definitely write Chris's neighbor a note. You're, like, the theater superstar here, so that would be so nice of you!

To Adam, I mean Greg, I mean Matt,

Matt. It's been such a long time since I've had to remember a Freshman's name, Pete. Ughhhhh. Sat. Cat. Matt. I will get it one of these days. I pinky promise.

Anyway, Matt . . . I thought I'd write you a folded note to welcome you to South High. My boyfriend slash your across-the-street neighbor, Christopher Caparelli, has told me lots about you. Well, I guess not lots. Just that you're named Matt (a name that's incredibly challenging to register) and that you like theater.

I hope to see you later at auditions. I'll be the girl with long blond hair (it's, like, down to my butt 'cuz I grew it out over the summer), and I will be singing "On My Own" from *Les Misérables*, and for my dance routine, well, let's just say I'll be doing a couple of splits, soooooooooo . . .

What are you gonna sing, Freshman Guy? Do you dance, too? What part do you want? Don't be bummed out if you only get chorus 'cuz it's beyond rare for a Freshman to get lead parts or even supporting. I'm gonna play Sandy. It's been a lifelong dream of mine. And there's no better way to start my Senior year than by getting one of the great roles in American theater, Derek.

Cat. Sat. Matt. Ughhh. I WILL REMEMBER YOUR NAME AT SOME POINT!!!!!!

Anyway, Matt . . . best of luck to you at auditions. Just be confident, know what I mean? Do you? Do you know what I mean?

Take care,
Tara Maureen Murphy

Dear Tara,

Thanks for writing me a note. Pretty awesome to get one from a Senior. Chris is an awesome guy. He even drove me to school this morning. That was pretty awesome because most of my friends took the bus except for people with older siblings at South. My brother is at Syracuse University this year, otherwise he would have driven me. Did you ever meet my brother? David Bloom? Heather Gould offered me a ride to school, too, but she makes everyone pay gas money, and when she misses a green light she says, "Shoulda-woulda-coulda," and when she sees a car with a headlight out she says, "Padiddle." So I said no.

I'm gonna sing "Dogs in the Yard" today. It's from the musical *Fame*. And yeah, I dance. I think I'm just gonna make up a dance routine when I get up there. I really want to play Danny Zuko. So, we'll see what happens.

How do you fold your notes like an envelope? That's pretty awesome.

Matt Bloom

Hey Mark (Sat, Cat . . . Matt)— hey Matt,

You say "pretty awesome" a lot. That's cute. Very Freshman-y. You'll learn more expressions now that you're at South. Just don't say MINT CONDITION. It's overused by average people. And whatever you do, never say KHED instead of KID. People around here think it's cool, but I've gotta tell you, it's not.

Danny Zuko?!!!!! That's the lead, Matt. You're in 9th grade. I mean, good luck and junk, but I've gotta be older-sister-ish and tell you that it's very impossible to beat out Ari Levy or Joel Waldman. I mean, those guys are Seniors, and they're majorly talented. But good for you for tryin'. I always say, "Aim for the moon," 'cuz in case you miss you'll be hangin' among the stars. Know what I mean? Do you? Do you know what I mean, Young Person?

Look at you askin' me how I fold my notes! Ever seen *Mystic Pizza*, Matt? If you haven't, you should. It's about a really hot girl and her weird friend and homely sister. The hot girl wants to get the hell outta her small town. She deserves to get out and live a better life. Anyway, she works at a pizza joint, and the fat woman who runs the joint makes the best pizza, but she won't tell anyone what's in the pizza. Not even the hot girl. Well, Matt. You probably think I'm the hot girl in this analogy, but guess what? I'm actually the fat woman with the top-secret pizza recipe. And double guess what? My folding is top secret, too.

I HATE HEATHER GOULD! I am so proud, in an older-sister way, that you turned down her offer to drive you to school. She's in marching band, Matt (which is a very hard thing to get into and very, veeery good for college transcripts), but she doesn't even play any instruments, she just twirls a baton! But because she's the baton twirler she's in the front row, so everyone sees her first at football games, so she thinks she's the best. And she always talks about marching band, but it's like, "Heather, you just throw a dumb stick around, you're not friggin' Mozart!"

And oh my god . . . she did a video presentation for Ms. Feeno's Spanish class last year where she played two characters (a Spanish-speaking Robin Leach and a Spanish-speaking Madonna, 'cuz in her video presentation Robin Leach was interviewing Madonna at one of her "mansions" for *Lifestyles of the Rich and Famous*), and she filmed it in her basement and by her aboveground pool and tried to pass it off as a mansion, not to mention it should be illegal for non-actresses slash baton twirlers who pretend to be in the marching band to play Madonna in ANYTHING! Have some friggin' respect. You gotta be someone with years of experience and natural chops to take on Madonna. So few of us can pull that off, do you know what I mean? I know you're fresh outta middle school and stuff, but do you know what I mean? Stay away from Heather Gould! K?

See ya at auditions. And you'll be so great in the chorus.

Always,

Tara Maureen Murphy

Dear Tara,

I like *Mystic Pizza* a lot. My mom's a teacher at another school, but sometimes she takes me out of school so we can play hooky together. We always do cool things like go into Harvard Square or Faneuil Hall. She took me to see *Mystic Pizza* at that small theater downtown. You know that one?

Leona. Leona is the woman who won't tell her pizza secrets. And Daisy is the hot girl in the movie.

Chorus would be cool, I guess. But I am going for Danny Zuko.

Hope you're having a friggin' great day
(new expression),
Matt Bloom

Dearest Christopher,

Q believe your little neighbor Ben, I mean Matt, is tryin' out for Danny Zuko? He's nuts. Freshmen never get leads, Christopher. You haven't even asked me if I'm nervous for auditions? Hello . . .

xoxo, I guess,
Tara

Hey T-Baby,

What's Danny Zuko? Yeah, Matty B. is a good kid. Super cool you're being cool to him. He told me. And I was like, "That's why she's my girl."

Crossing my fingers for you, Tara. Kick ass. And when you're done with your audition get in your Wagoneer and get on over to my house. Mom's out of town as usual, so the kitchen counter is all ours.

Love ya,
C.P.C.

Dear Christopher,

What's Danny Zuko?!!!!!!!
    Maybe I'll come over later. Maybe.

Mwah,
Tara

To Stefanie,

Sorry it's taken me so long to write you back. As you can imagine, there was a ton of new information in your note, and someone like me, a very, veeery deep and loving person, needs time to process new information, especially when it involves my best friend on earth. That would be you, Stef. Not like you don't remember, but just a reminder in case.

First let me tell you that I did write a welcome note to that Freshman across-the-street neighbor of Christopher's. And he seems sweet, young, and a bit naive. He is auditioning for Danny Zuko, and we all know that Freshmen never get lead roles, but he doesn't seem to care about facts. Anyway, I share this with you because of the FACT that you are my best friend and we have always shared EVERYTHING with each other. Do you know what I mean, Stef?

So you sew! Wowie Zowie a-zing-a-zang-zong. Remember that expression from when we were in second grade and we would walk around the neighborhood after playing kick the can in the SUMMER?

Summer. Ahhh, the season SANDWICHED between spring and fall.

You mentioned me coming to your cottage on Nantucket! Amazing. When? I need dates, as my Month-At-A-Glance is getting very, veeery full.

You have certainly made me wicked curious about the seven weeks that followed your learning-how-to-sew day at Stacey Simon's oceanfront house. Was that the last time you saw her? Did she wear her famous jean jacket all summer? Did you confront her about always being a bitch to me? I'm sure you confronted her and told her how conceited she is and how she has been so very rude (ARE-YOU-D-E) to your necklace-splitting BFF. That would be ME. Just sayin'.

You said "on island" a ton. Do people on Nantucket use the word THE? ON THE ISLAND. Or is THE more of an OFF ISLAND kinda word?

I did save my old sheets, and I will absolutely think about your offer to sew them into something else.

I have auditions tomorrow and will obviously be booked super solid with my boyfriend (C.P. Caparelli) over the weekend, but call me. Oh wait, are you guys allowed to use your IN TOWN phone or are you still staying "present"?

I love you sew much . . .

Tara

Dear Matt,

See, I remembered your name.

Matt, I was moved to write you this note because I've never seen a Freshman boy be so amazin' on that stage. I love that song—"Dogs in the Yard"—but I never got it until you sang it. The way you interpreted those lyrics . . . I was like, "I wonder what this very young boy wants in life? He seems to have many a story to tell, which is a most rare thing in this town. So he wants to go crazy, he passionately sings, much like dogs do in yards. Does he want to rip off his 'collar' and hop the suburban fence? What is it he wants?" See, an audition such as yours makes a tried-and-true super-talent such as me ask the deeper questions. Wow, Matt! Just wow. Kudos to you. And you're a real good dancer, too, Matt.

I had a vision that you were Danny and I was Sandy. But even if you don't get the part I will never forget that audition, Matt.

And hey, what was up with you and Joy Bernstein? I, like, saw you guys flirtin'? Do you have a crush on her? Are you sleepin' with her, Matt? Joy is very calculating, Matt. Just be careful. She thinks 'cuz her hair is long and curly that she's better than people. And she's only a Sophomore. Do you like her voice?

Very, veeeeerrrry good job today. Your big sister is very proud.

Be good,

Tara (Maureen Murphy)

Dear Tara,

Thanks a lot. You thinking I was good at auditions means a lot, especially coming from you because you're Chris's girlfriend and your opinion means a lot. Also, you were pretty awesome—I mean very good—up there. And your dance was amazing. Was that Irish step?

I just met Joy Bernstein today. We weren't flirting. Just talking. Her hair is really long and super curly. Kinda like Daisy's from *Mystic Pizza*. Um, yeah. I think her voice is amazingly good.

That would be awesome if you were Sandy and I was Danny. Chris's neighbor and his girlfriend playing the leads in *Grease*?! Cool!! I guess we'll find out tomorrow morning.

Good luck!

Your little brother,
Matt (Bloom)

MATT!!!!

OH MY GOD!!! "I'm Joy Rebecca Bernstein, and I hoodwink directors and bamboozle theater systems so I can steal parts that belong to Tara Maureen Murphy!" That conniving little girl-child is trying to make me look bad. We get it, Joy! You can sing to the back of the theater . . . This just in, hon . . . doesn't mean the back of the theater is likin' what they're hearin'!! Only in this town would directors think louder is better. I'm a friggin' SENIOR, Matt! I'm Tara Maureen Murphy!! Co-captain of the cheerleaders and a theater star. And you're tellin' me I am playing Patty Simcox?!!!? Patty friggin' Simcox???? She's like the Heather Gould of characters. Ahhhhhhhhhhhh! I hate it here!! I'm way too big for this town.

Oh, and congratulations, Matt. You will be a great Danny Zuko.

Tara

OCTOBER 1991

T-baby,

I'm wicked sorry about last night. My answering machine broke, so I didn't even know you called. I was just playing street hockey with Tzoug and Dube. And obviously talkin' about you. But I didn't hear my phone ringing 'cuz I was outside.

I gotta take a friggin' Spanish test today, which sucks ball sack. *Hola* and *jugar al tenis* can kiss my *culo*. I wish we could take Canadian instead of Spanish 'cuz at least they have hockey so I could communicate if I moved there.

Oh, Friday night Perroni's parents are outta town and she's having a bender. I say we go. We going?

Peace in the Middle East.

You're the tits.

Love you, baby,
C.P.C.

Chris,

Your answering machine broke?!?!?!?!?!?!?!? Oh, I'm soooo sorry to hear that, Chris. I just hate when answering machines break, because then you don't know that your girlfriend called 30 friggin' times because she was crying because she was WICKED UPSET ABOUT A TON OF THINGS!!!!!!

I'm so glad you got to play street hockey with Tzoug and Dube. But I'm pretty sure they don't bake you gooey double-chocolate-chip cookies and grab your crotch at the movies. So maybe, JUST MAYBE, you can start bein' a little more thoughtful and, oh I don't know . . . how do you say it in Canadian . . . CALL YOUR GIRLFRIEND!!!!!! Seriously?! It's 1991, Caparelli! Get a clue!

You don't even know what's goin' on in my life, Christopher. Did you even know that I started wearin' Trésor? And do you even know WHY I started wearin' Trésor? NO.

I was at rehearsal yesterday, and as I was twirlin' my friggin' Patty Simcox-Gould baton, Joy Rebecca Bernstein danced by, and guess what, Christopher? I got a whiff of her. And double guess what, Christopher? She was WEARIN' Anaïs Anaïs. MY FRAGRANCE!!!!

32

That girl has literally taken everything from me. Last year, she had the nerve to get Marianne Paroo in *The Music Man* (a part that I could literally play in my sleep), and this year, she steals my dream role from me. In what alternate universe is Sandy from *Grease* a Jewish girl with long, curly hair? How is that even possible, Christopher? And I'm sorry, everyone, but her hair looks like a friggin' owl's nest. Like some baby-beaked, big-eyed, neck-turnin' night bird is gonna peek out any friggin' minute! Only in this town do people find that kinda hair awesome. My hair is longer than hers when I brush it out!

Speakin' of brushing out, did you even know that I got a new hairbrush because I threw mine against a cinderblock wall after Joy walked by me smelling of Anaïs Anaïs!??!? No. You didn't. Lately I feel like you don't even know me anymore. And that makes me painfully sad. 'Cuz I do love you and we are a Supercouple, but it's October, C.P.C. The leaves are startin' to change. The air is gettin' crisper. Halloween's around the corner. It's like time's flyin' by. We're only gonna be Seniors once, Christopher. This is our last autumn together in this town. Do you even get that? Do you?

So anyway, now I wear Trésor. No one else better start wearin' it or I'm gonna be so mad. I will not wear EXCLAMATION, but I guess I like Benetton Colors. That's not even the point, Christopher!!!!

In three weeks I will be onstage, opening night of *Grease*! And I will be twirlin' a goddamn baton as Bernstein plays the part that should have been mine. She has taken so very much from me. She messed with the wrong girl. Are you gonna come to opening night? I mean, you don't call me, so how am I APPOSED to know? And if you do come, Chris, are you comin' to support me or your idiot neighbor, Ronald? The hell is that loser's name? Met? Mort?

I hate this town right now. I've done so much for this place, and this is the thanks I get?! Don't even talk to me about Stef! Ahhhhhhhhhhh!!!!! Okay. Deep breath.

Put this note up to your nose, Christopher. I spritzed it with my new perfume 'cuz with you not callin' me last night I figured how the heck do I know when I'll see you again, so I wanted to share, as proper girlfriends do, what I smell like these October days.

Hope you get your "answering machine" fixed!

Hearts and Stars,
Tara

To-est MY BEST FRIEND!

Tara, come on! You have to talk to me. Ever since I told you about my summer on Nantucket you've ignored me in the hallways, and I think you tripped me when we were walking out of Ms. Maderos's class. Maybe you didn't trip me, but I fell over a foot and it wasn't my foot, and when I looked up you were kind of smiling. Did you trip me? Oh my god, what is happening with us? This is Senior year, Tara. It's not supposed to be going like this.

At least talk to me and share your feelings with me. You've always shared everything with me, and now you're like a stranger.

No one will ever replace you. I split one necklace in my whole life, and that was with you.

You know me, Tara! I'm not the girl who goes around ditching my best friend for the popular, pretty girl! You know I'm not like that.

How can we get through this? I miss you. I miss Triple *L*. I miss us. My life has been so different without you in it. It's all so . . . I don't even know what to say.

How are you? How is your world?

Love you Muchly and Moreso,

Stef "Minnie Strone, Tomato, Split Pea Soup" Campbell

Hello Stef,

'Sup? Let me clear the incredibly thick, polluted, storm-cloud-filled air that you and I have been breathin' since you arrived back on the mainland.

To go forward, let us first go back in time. Care to jump in my DeLorean, Stef?

When I was a little girl, I was in Ms. Bugg's kindergarten class. You had Ms. Butler, remember? I know kindergarten was a million years ago, but I remember it like it was yesterday. I will never forget the movable wall they had between Bugg's and Butler's rooms. We would get wicked excited on that rare occasion they would open the wall. You and I would run as fast as we could into each other's arms.

I will never forget me punching Jonathan Casey in the ear 'cuz he threw a grape juice box at your head. I still don't believe I was the one who gave him cauliflower ear 'cuz he was always wrestling with people and, like, every wrestler gets that vegetable-ear thing, but anyway I punched him 'cuz I was defendin' you. No one messed with you on my Swatch watch, Steffed Animal!

And who can forget Balloon Day? Not this girl!!

Stef, Stacey Simon popped my balloon on Balloon Day, forever destroying my chance at winning the prize. How could I win a gift certificate to Tony Roma's if my balloon could never fly up into the air, carrying my postcard, and then deflate and land on someone's yard or driveway or car? And if you can jog your memory you will recall that Stacey Simon won that year, which I still marvel at and find very, veeery interesting slash curious. Really, her balloon won? Or did her rich parents rig the system? They did get a plaque that same year in the library, which leads me and my mom to believe the Simons paid off the school so that bitch could win Balloon Day! I'm certain if I had won and gotten that gift certificate I could've taken my mom and dad to Tony Roma's for a wicked nice dinner and things could've been different for them. And that wasn't the only "balloon" of mine Stacey Simon popped, and you know it!

Our Freshman year ski trip to Killington! We were on the chairlift right behind Stacey Simon, and right when her lift was about to get to the ski-off she FELL OFF! Really? She fell off the friggin' chairlift and who came running to her rescue? Robbie the chairlift operator, who just happened to be the hottest guy in Vermont, who just happened to be the one guy on that entire mountain I said I liked!! An entire mountain, Stef! So much terrain with thousands of cute guys and she had to fall for Robbie the chairlift operator? Not to mention she had to know I was afraid of heights and we were left danglin' in the air for an hour while Princess Stacey got rescued by my Robbie, who just one run earlier said "Awesome Oakleys" to me. The story of her going to the hospital was absolute hogwarsh (as my gramma used to say). You and I both know she hooked up with him just to mess with me even more.

And last but so not least was that time Sophomore year when I was gonna move to New York City. You weren't in our English class, Stef, but oh man do you know the story as well as I do.

Mr. Donovan kindly told the class that I would be bidding this town farewell for the bright lights of Manhattan, and in front of everyone Stacey Simon had the audacity to say, "That's so awesome, Tara. What part of the city?" And in my head I was like, "Hmm, who do I currently think is hot that Stacey Simon must want to steal from me and hook up with? Hmmm." And as you and I both know, those were the first of my Timmy Garabino days, Stef! And he was, drumroll please . . . HOT! Shocker! So I just simply said, "Downtown." To which she publicly replied, "Cool. Where?" And I was like, duh, you idiot . . . DOWNTOWN! So I said, "Um . . . downtown!" She was like, "The East Side? Lower East Side? The West Village? Tribeca? Wall Street?" Yeah, Stef . . . like I was gonna move to Wall Street so I could be a friggin' stockbroker. I was like, "West Village." And she was like, "I love it there. I have family who lives on West 12th Street and 8th Avenue." I was like, "Well, they're gonna be my new neighbors 'cuz I'm moving to West 12th Street and 2nd Avenue." And what did Stacey Simon say? "I think that's the East Village." Then she laughed. It was like I was in a hot air balloon flyin' right over this cruel town and she took her bow and arrow and popped it.

That is Stacey Simon, Stef. Under that jean jacket is a girl with needles for fingers.

How are you friends with our mortal enemy?! 'Cuz of some sewing machine? 'Cuz you were ON ISLAND together? Are you kidding me??!!

How is my world, you ask? There's so much goin' on and so much of it is just wicked intense.

I never imagined a world where I would NOT be Sandy in *Grease*. I was her for Halloween five years in a row. I deserved to be her! I don't know. I just don't know!

And things with C.P.C. are fine. We are definitely one of the rare couples in this town, but again I don't know. I just don't know, you know?

And this Freshman kid, you know Christopher's across-the-street neighbor (now, in a parallel universe, also known as Danny Zuko) is really drivin' me nuts. Here's this kid who just arrived—A FRESHMAN—and he's just disruptin' the natural order of things.

My world. How is my world? I'm sure you've smelled me in the halls when I've rushed by you (busy, busy, busy), and yes, that's Trésor. Long story I will tell you if we hang out. IF.

Best wishes,

Tara M. Murphy

Dear the most beautiful girl in the world,

I AM SERIOUSLY SORRY I DIDN'T CALL YOU LAST NIGHT! See, I spelled that in all capital letters, so you know I mean it.

That girl Joy may have gotten your part and taken your perfume, but she's got nothin' on you, T. You have bigger gazongas, anyway.

You pissed at Matty B.? Is he being a dick to you, 'cuz if he is I'm gonna have to say somethin' to him. Let me know.

I'm just gonna buy a new answering machine after school. Hey, I have an idea. How about you come over after rehearsal and record my answering machine greeting for me? I'd like that. Why? 'Cuz you're my girlfriend.

I smelled your note. Just me or does Trésor smell like sex? Me likesy.

Love ya, baby,
C.P.C.

To-est T. Murphs—

I will still write "To-est" to you no matter what. That is our official greeting, and I know you know that.

I have noticed you changed your perfume. I mean, at first it was hard to tell because you were basically sprinting by me—I was like, "Is she training for a marathon?"—but after a few times I figured that yes, you had changed your fragrance. I love Trésor, but I LOVE IT ON YOU THE MOST.

Your life sounds really heavy right now, and I know what that feels like, and I am so sorry you're hurting right now.

You absolutely should have gotten Sandy! That is outrageous, and I feel like everyone knows it. I KNOW IT, and that's all that matters. You are a gift to the theater, Tara. You are a true actress. And this Joy girl is a flash in the pan. There's no way she is as talented as you. But I'm sorry you didn't get the part. You were born to be Sandy.

As for Stacey . . . I think your history with her might actually be slightly different than what you've thought.

The balloon-day conspiracy is complicated, I'll give you that. I've always said I never actually saw Stacey pop your balloon, but you are right I never disputed *your* theory on that. Maybe she did. Maybe she didn't. But who she is now is not who she was when we were five. And I know how much you wanted to take your parents to Tony Roma's, but I've told you this a million times and will tell you a million more . . . you are not the reason for any of their "stuff." If anything, Tara, you are the reason they are still working hard to make it work.

And I don't want you to think that I'm defending Stacey, but Tara . . . she did fall off the chairlift and her knee did pop out. She did go to the hospital, and she was on crutches for, like, three months. I'm your best friend, and I was the only one who knew you were scared of heights, and I was also the only one who knew you had a crush on the chairlift operator guy.

And I know how badly you wanted to move away and go to New York. Selfishly I half loved that time because you slept over almost every night, and it was like we lived together, and I loved that more than anything. My parents loved it, too. The other half of me hated it because of everything going on at your house. And no, I was not in Mr. Donovan's class, but from what I heard Stacey didn't laugh at you. That foul animal Dougie Fitz blew a boogie on Jessica Klein's back and HE laughed. He also got suspended. And from what I heard Stacey offered you her aunt and uncle's phone number in case you needed anything in New York . . . you know, when you moved there.

After spending so much time with her on Nantucket I realized Stacey Simon isn't at all what we thought, Tara. She doesn't think of herself as popular and doesn't wake up and stare in the mirror going, "I am the most beautiful person in town." She's actually very insecure about stuff. She thinks everyone HATES HER. I know, shocking.

She struggles just like us. She and Justin have a ton of problems and have broken up a bunch without anyone ever knowing. She tries very hard to keep her private life private, but I told her that is hard when everyone makes up ideas about her or spreads rumors about her which then everyone thinks are trumors. She is even considering not going to Prom because she doesn't want for her and Justin to win Prom queen and king because she thinks people will . . . well . . . that they'll think the system is rigged in her favor. Stacey feels like no one in this town has ever understood her. I can relate to that. Can you? I think you can, Tara. I know you, and I think you can relate to that.

Stacey, who did wear her famous jean jacket a lot over the summer, asked if the three of us could hang out. Would you be open to that? Would you give her a chance? Would you give me a chance?

And I was thinking, you know . . . if you are willing to let me teach you how to sew that we could make matching purses out of your hearts-and-stars sheets. You know, like, the next version of our BEST FRIEND NECKLACE. Think about it?

Mwah, Miss Trésor.

Muchly and Moreso,
Soup

To Whom It May Concern a.k.a. my boyfriend Christopher Caparelli's across-the-street neighbor a.k.a. you are a FRESHMAN so DON'T YOU FORGET IT—

Hey, a few things, Marty . . .

I wanted to cut something off at the pass, hon. Christopher is very, veeeerry upset right now 'cuz he has heard, as people at South High tend to do, that you are bein' a little bit conceited since you got the lead in *Grease*. I have tried to calm him down, but he's just really mad that you are acting different. It's almost like you think you're the real Danny Zuko. Well, that's what people are sayin', anyway. You are very young and impressionable. I can see that now. And yes, Matt, you have a great theatrical voice and sure you can dance super good, but that does not necessarily mean you're a star.

I am and will continue to talk Christopher off the ledge. He wants to confront you, but I'm tryin' to stop that from happenin'. And he listens to me, Matt. And you know I'm like your big sister, so I am just lookin' out for you here.

I'm gonna first tell you about stars. Not the ones in the sky, Silly Young Person. Though I do love lyin' on a blanket in Camel Lot and stargazin'. You don't even know what Camel Lot is, Matt. And you might never know. 'Cuz it's my special place where I go to think about all the chaos this town brings my way. It would take the specialest person in the world to experience Camel Lot with this girl.

Back to stars. A star is a person who carries themself with dignity. A star is someone who can sing, act, dance, and BE A GOOD PERSON. And be SMART ABOUT THEIR CHOICES.

I'm a star, Matt. Wanna know why? 'Cuz I'm incredibly talented (national cheerleading finalist three years in a row, lead in MOST of the plays when certain non-Catholic bitches don't get in the way, and a very dignified, kind person).

I will be leaving this town in less than a calendar year, and I will most likely be leavin' it forever. There's nothing here for me, Matt. Besides my super athletic, gorgeous boyfriend, C.P.C. But he will visit me on Broadway. You heard of Broadway, Matt? It's this very important place where STARS end up. You could end up there too, Matt . . . but if you keep flyin' too close to the sun you're gonna get burned.

What is it about your fascination with this Joy Rebecca Bernstein? Just because she's playin' Sandy and you're playin' Danny does not mean you have to hang out with her. It's a very, verrrrry Freshman-y thing you're doing, hanging out with Joy. I know you think that if you spend private time together you will give a better performance come show night. But that's a myth, Matt.

In order for me to protect you from Christopher's wrath (he has a dark side when pushed) and to keep your reputation intact, I would suggest you let me in. Let me into your world.

Look, if you're sleeping with Joy, you can tell me. And if you are havin' a sexual dalliance with her, I am prayerful that she treats you with the respect you so deserve.

And are you aware that Joy is now wearing my fragrance? I'm not mad about it. It's just perfume. Like, I don't even care at all, buuuuuut it's all very, veeeerry curious, do you know what I mean?

Anyway, I am here to protect you the way only a big sis could.

I look forward to your response. I promise to keep Christopher calm until I hear from you.

Fondly,
Tara Maureen Murphy . . . SENIOR!

Dear Tara,

I just read your note. How did you get it into my backpack? I'm not mad, I just didn't even see you put it in there.

Let me start off by saying thank you soooooooooooooooo ooooooooooooooooooo much for telling Chris I'm not being conceited. I really appreciate that.

I didn't even realize I was acting differently. I still don't know exactly what I'm doing that's different, but I definitely don't want people to think I'm cocky. I hate conceited people, so I don't want to be one of them.

You have been so nice to me since I got to South High. I will never forget that for the rest of my whole life.

I never want to bother you at rehearsals because you're always with the other Seniors, and, I don't know, I guess I feel a little uncomfortable because it seems like Joel Waldman and Ari Levy hate me because I got Danny Zuko and they didn't. My mom and dad always raised me and my brother to do our best and go for our dreams, so I went for mine. I never meant to make anyone hate me. I wasn't trying to take a part from them. But anyway, I always see you hanging out with them, and it feels like I shouldn't interrupt you guys.

I've become really good friends with Joy. She just gets me. She does all these funny voices, and we have a bunch of inside jokes. Like our own language. That probably seems dumb to you 'cuz it's kind of immature, but maybe it's just 'cuz we're younger so we like it. I gave her that perfume as a show present. She gave me Drakkar Noir, so my mom took me to the store to get Joy a perfume. I didn't know which one to buy, but then I smelled Anaïs Anaïs and it smelled good and familiar, so I bought her it. But now that I'm thinking about it, maybe it smelled familiar 'cuz you wear it and maybe I smelled it on you. So thank you for being the inspiration for Anaïs Anaïs perfume. Joy loves the perfume soooo much. It smells awesome on her.

I really think it is so cool that you're like my big sister 'cuz with my brother being at Syracuse and pledging Phi Kappa Psi he never even has time to talk on the phone so I can never ask him stuff right now. But I do have a crush on Joy. We haven't had sex, but we did make out the other night, which was really awesome. I am thinking that I want to ask her out, like to be my girlfriend, but I'm nervous because what if she said no and then we have to be in love in *Grease* (which opens in like three weeks, which is crazy).

So what do you think I should do? Just ask her out? Or just keep hooking up but date other people?

And are you sure I shouldn't talk to Chris so he knows that I'm not being conceited?

Thank YOU SOOOO MUCH, YOU ARE AN AWESOME OLDER SISTER!

Matt

P.S. I totally understand what you mean about being a star.

P.P.S. Camel Lot sounds so awesome. If I ask Joy out should I take her there to do it? Where is it?

Dear my angel, Christopher,

I will come over to your house tonight, and I will record your answering machine greeting. Because I love you more than life itself, Christopher.

I'm just sittin' here in calculus, and I was thinkin' about you . . . naked. I can't wait to kiss you later!

Your Girlfriend,
Tara

T—

I know I told you this last night, but I gotta say it one more time: YOU ARE THE SEXIEST GIRL ON EARTH. Probably Mars, too.

You are such a good person.

I used my mom's line to call my line just so I could hear your voice on my greeting. And then I had a solo mission.

Love ya,
C.P.C.

Dear Young Freshman
Matthew Bloom,

I am really gettin' a handle on your name, Matt, and I was wondering if I may call you Matthew. I think it suits you better as it is more of a statement. Matthew. Matt. See what I mean?

Look at you buying Anaïs Anaïs for Joy. I'm very flattered that I inspired that fragrance choice. Smells are a funny thing, Matthew. They define moments and memories. I don't love Drakkar Noir (no offense), as my ex-boyfriend, Timmy Garabino, wore it, and every time I smell it I remember our breakup. It was a very, veeerry intense breakup, Matthew. I don't usually talk about it, but seein' as you shared with me your crush on Joy and other very intimate details about your sex life, I find it only fair to start lettin' you in on my world.

Timmy graduated South High some years back. He was an exceptional lover. He had the biggest . . . well, he was a big boy, Matthew. It's not like I've been with a lot of guys 'cuz I haven't at all. I am no Kathy Connery! Don't get me wrong, she's a sweet girl and I've known her since nursery school, but she had a three-way with Steve Mazulo and Billy Moriarty and they're total skids (people who smoke pot behind the school and won't ever become anything). I am not a slut. I am a romantic girl stuck in a town that has no concept of romance.

Timmy and I were at the reservoir (I hate when people call it "the rez," reducing it to somethin' trashy when in fact it's quite beautiful, especially in a town where strip malls with places called Wicked Good Nails and Wicked Good Shoes and Wicked Great Bagels make up the bulk of the geography), and things definitely went in a different direction than I had thought, and I have the best perception-compass, so you can imagine how shocked I was. Especially 'cuz I was wearin' Timmy's Drakkar Noir–doused flannel. Boys don't let just anyone wear their flannels or jackets. Everyone knows that. Do you know that, Matthew? Never ever let just any girl wear your flannel or jacket unless you have love in your heart. K?

So anyway . . . we had been goin' out for a while, and I just got caught up in the moment, Matthew. Who wouldn't? The sun was goin' down, which made the reservoir glimmer like a sea of diamonds, and the early springtime breeze was just right. Not too strong, not too weak. Just enough to blow my extremely long hair (it was longer than it is now even—I know, crazy, right?) right onto my lips, and a lot of it got stuck on my Lip Smackers (Dr Pepper, as I know you're wonderin'). I was like basically a cat for a minute (tee-hee, tee-hee), no, but seriously, a few pieces got in my mouth, like in my throat, so I was literally a cat for a minute, no joke . . . but Timmy . . . he didn't skip a beat. Nope. He just took his hands and unstuck my hair from my lips. I pulled the pieces from my mouth, and he just looked at me the way a boy looks at a girl when he loves her. It was as romantic as it gets for a Sophomore girl dating a Senior guy. I felt it. I knew it. So I said it. I said, "I know. I love you, too." He smiled and stared at me and then he said, "Let's get goin'."

We got in his Volvo, and I was in my head thinkin', "Oh my god . . . is he takin' me to Ken's SteakHouse? Is he takin' me to see *Say Anything*? Where is this boy taking me??" And you know where he took me, Matthew? Home. We got to my house, he pulled into my driveway, and he said, "Take care." And I said, "Of what?" And he said, "Of you."

He then reached over me and unlocked my door. I didn't move, I couldn't. I didn't understand what was happening. I was young, world-weary, immature. Then he reached over me again and opened my door. I got out, and that was that. The last time I saw Timmy Garabino.

Was I sad? Sure. Of course I was, Matthew—I'm not a Nintendo game, I'm a human girl. But I'm also Tara Maureen Murphy, so what did I do? I threw myself into my acting. I got an amazing supporting role in *A Chorus Line* (Connie Wong), but bein' me I turned it into a major role. I chopped my hair off to be Connie Wong (the things real actresses do, right?), and I once again found true happiness in the theater.

Do I still have that flannel? Yes. But it's sealed in a bag, and it's in my Sophomore year box. Needless to say, Drakkar Noir makes me sick, so definitely do what you want but DO NOT wear it around me. K? Also, I'm not sayin' Joy doesn't have class, but Drakkar isn't the classiest fragrance around.

Everything makes sense when you grow up, Matthew. Like now, the thought of someone like me dating someone like Timmy Garabino is absolutely absurd. I mean, Timmy compared to Christopher? Fool's gold. Hilarious. There is no comparison.

And while Christopher is a very good guy (and I find him beyond attractive), I'm gonna tell you somethin', Matthew, and you gotta promise you will never say anything . . . ready????????? Chris is kinda boring me.

I need someone smart and interesting. Someone who makes me laugh. Someone who will have inside jokes with me. Someone I can, like, have my own language with. Do you know anyone in this town like that? And I mean, besides you 'cuz you're into Joy and it's not like I like you that way . . . oh my god, I pray you didn't think that because I would feel so embarrassed for you for thinkin' that. I DO NOT LIKE YOU. YOU ARE A FRESHMAN and NOT MY TYPE AT

ALL. So please, if you were hopin' I had a crush on you, get that out of your head, Matthew. The thought of kissing you makes me Drakkar Noir sick.

I'm sorry I didn't respond to you sooner, but let me take this opportunity to address some of your questions about the love of your life, Joy Rebecca Bernstein.

Well, first of all, have you ever had sex? Are you a virgin? What bases have you gone to? I need hard information in order to be the best big sister possible. What kind of kisser are you? Aggressive or passionate?

And NO, YOU CANNOT TAKE JOY TO CAMEL LOT! How dare you even suggest that. Camel Lot became my secret place after that day at the reservoir. And I will gladly write out directions to that place for you! Just remember . . . never call it "the rez." Only low-class people say that, Matthew.

Write me back ASAP.

Oh, and I've calmed Christopher down. He is not mad at you right now.

Big Sis,
Tara

Dear Tara,

I'm really sorry I suggested asking Joy out at Camel Lot. I will never do that again. My bad. Will you maybe show me it one day? We can lay on a blanket and talk about life and our dreams.

I would say I'm a passionate kisser. I love kissing slowly and then a little faster. You might think this is weird, but girls like to bite on my lips, I guess 'cuz I have big lips. I haven't done too much, but I've felt girls up and dry humped Jill Kablotzky at overnight camp. I am a virgin, but don't tell anyone 'cuz it's kinda embarrassing. But if I ask Joy out and she says yes, I think I will lose my virginity with her.

I didn't think you had a crush on me. That would be crazy anyway 'cuz you're going out with Chris and he's my neighbor.

Anyway. See you at rehearsal later, and THANK GOD IT'S FRIDAY!!

Your Bro,
Matthew

Matthew,

So you've felt girls up? I'm assuming that you've done so over the shirt, correct? So basically in reality you've never felt breasts before. I have very, verrrrry big breasts so it takes some big hands to cup mine. Do you have big hands? I've never looked at them. Do you even have hands, Matthew? I guess I've never really looked at you like looked at you looked at you, you know what I mean?

It's not embarrassin' that you're a virgin. It's kinda sweet. I really suggest you lose your virginity to someone who cares deeply about you. Someone you can trust. Someone who loves you. You deserve to be loved. Do you know that?

I lost my virginity to Kev Brandolini. He didn't even go to South High. He went to boarding school, but he was from here. I was a Freshman (seems like light years ago), and Kev was home for Christmas break. I was with my mom, pickin' up last-minute ornaments at the Christmas Tree Shop. It was soooooooooooo cold outside. You know how winter can be. I could smell hot cocoa in the air, and wanna know why? Because Kev Brandolini was drinkin' hot cocoa, and he was standin' right next to me. He was there pickin' up tinsel for one of his

Christmas trees. His family lives up by Faffard Lane. You know those mansions? They have horses, too. And they have tons of Christmas trees. Imagine that. Bein' so rich you have tons of Christmas trees. His house was so pretty. All those twinklin' lights. Anyway, Kev was there, and he was so hot and tall. He had one of those preppy haircuts where it's, like, longer on the top and shaved around the sides and back. He was wearing a baseball hat, but his long hair in the front was sticking out. And he said, "You're Tara Murphy, right?" And I was like, "Yeah." And he was like, "I saw you in the newspaper for cheerleading."

The squad had just come back from Nashville, where we came in second at Nationals. And there was a huge picture of us on the front page. Kev asked me if I liked Christmas and I told him that I lived for Christmas, and he asked me if I wanted to see all their trees and I said YES. Kev picked me up that night. Oh my god, Matthew, he drove the coolest jeep ever!!

So, he took me to his mansion and the trees were gorgeous. And Kev showed me his room, and it had tons of trophies from lacrosse, and he asked me if he could kiss me. And I was tremblin', but I let him. And we sort of hung out for the rest of Christmas break and ended up having sex in the horse stables. And then, like a flash, Kev Brandolini was gone, back to boarding school. Like he just sorta disappeared. He never called me after that, and now he's in college somewhere, but I will never forget him.

To be loved has gotta be the most incredible feelin' in the world. Real love. True love. I don't know that I've ever been loved like REALLY LOVED. Have you? Did Jill Kablotzky LOVE you? Or any of the other girls you've hooked up with?

Don't get me wrong, Christopher Caparelli and I are one of the greatest Supercouples this town has ever seen, but somethin' is missin'. I long for the day when I feel so in love that my heart bursts like a firework on the Fourth of July.

Hang on a sec. I'm gonna brush my hair with my new brush. My hair is so long right now I'm like Rapunzel and Madison from *Splash*. Eek Eek Eek Eek. Hang on.

Ok. I brushed it. I think it grew an inch since we started *Grease* rehearsals. Q even believe that?

Do you like when I spray my bangs up or when I curl them over my forehead?

Anyway, Matt (I actually like callin' you Matt sometimes 'cuz it takes less time to say than Matthew. Don't get me wrong, Matthew is a much more proper name, but Matt is just quicker and I don't always or usually have a ton of time to reference you 'cuz I'm a Senior and have tons of obligations socially and academically and extracurricularly). But as I was sayin', Matt . . . is Joy a Kev Brandolini? Like, is she gonna make love to you and then skip town? You know what I mean?

Think about it. I know you're a bright young kid, so I have no doubt you will make the smartest CHOICE. It's no joke bein' in high school. I mean, yeah, in middle school you could mess around and be stupid, but this is real life now. Every move we make is important.

I'm gonna leave you with this, Kiddo. Season. Reason. Lifetime. Those words seem very simple at first blush, but go deeper. People are in our lives for a season. A reason. Or a lifetime.

What's Joy, Matt? Once you know the answer to that, you will know whether or not you should ask her to be your girlfriend.

Alright, Pipsqueak. I gotta brush my hair some more 'cuz it is sooooooo verrrry long and cumbersome if I don't brush the crap outta it. And yes, Matt—Thank God It Is Friday. I have a party to attend this evening at Nikki Perroni's home. She is pretty cool but has been known to be a klepto at many stores. Word is she switches tags out so she, like, buys stuff but for much cheaper than it usually is. I don't even want to go to this stupid party, but Christopher does so I will.

Take the weekend to think things over. Season. Reason. Lifetime. And write me first thing Monday mornin'. You can always slip notes in my locker if you fold 'em tight enough.

Be good, you,
Tara Maureen

To-est Cream of Mushroom (new one!)—

Oh my dearest sister slash soul mate slash sometimes-daughter (when I protect you like a mama bear)—I just adore you, you BB Minkey. No one else has created a language like we have. Minkey instead of Monkey. Q even instead of Can You Even. SOOF (swear on our friendship), SOML (swear on my life), BB instead of Baby, BB Minkey instead of Baby Monkey, and the list goes on and on, My Girl of Girls.

Miss Trésor (tee-hee, tee-hee)—that brought a smile to my face. It is kinda funny just the absurdness of it all. Ahhhhh, LIFE!!

You know, Stef, things are kinda lookin' up. New day, new chance at finding happiness in a town not very known for happiness.

I think, for now, we will just put a pin in the Balloon Day events. Maybe it wasn't Stacey Simon after all. And who even cares, right? Look, whoever popped that balloon has some serious "Karma (Chameleon)" on their hands, but that's their story, not ours. And as for the ski trip . . . water under the Bourne Bridge. And I have a vague memory of Dougie Fitz that day in Mr. Donovan's class (who can forget a pig person blowing a boogie on an innocent girl's back?!). Anyway . . . all that nonsense is wicked in the past, as we are college bound. I am X'ing out days in my Month-At-A-Glance. NYU, here I come!! I mean, I of course want to get in everywhere else, but is there really any other place like NYU for me? I'll answer that. No!!

So, Stacey Simon wants to hang out the three of us? Wow. What has she said? How many times has she asked? Gotta say, I'm impressed. She knows that the only way to properly know you is to know your best friend. That's cool. Good for her. You know what, cutes . . . okay!! I would like nothin' more than to put history in the books. We are all Seniors, and that's sayin' a lot. So, yeah, Stef. Yeah. Let's hang out with Stacey Simon.

But first, I thought you should know I pulled my hearts-and-stars sheets from the attic, and they are waiting for us to make our matching pock-a-books. I even told Christopher that I have to blow off Nikki Perroni's party tonight (you were probably goin' too, but who cares, right?) to hang out with my best friend. Wanna just skip the party and hang out in my room and . . . sew? That way, come Monday, we will have our matchin' pock-a-books? And besides, we need just us time! Bring your Month-At-A-Glance so we can calendar a proper time with Stace. Does feel like a very powerful trio: me, you, and Stacey Simon. Senior year is full of surprises!

So? What do ya say?

All my love . . .

T-Murphs, Tmurphette, Tara Maureen

To-est Tar—

Yes! Consider the party blown off! I am coming to your house, sewing machine in hand. Will need your help unloading it from my trunk but can't wait.

Want to order Chinese? Oh, and I will definitely bring my calendar. I told Stacey we are going to all hang out, and she is thrilled!

So thankful we have cleared that "polluted, storm-cloud-filled air."

Love you, BB Minkey,

Muchly and Moreso,
Stef

To-est Soup!!

I have been gettin' so many compliments on my pock-a-book. People are like, "Where did you buy that—it's so cool and different!" I'm like, "Me and Stef Campbell sewed them," and everyone freaks out.

I knew walkin' into school this morning with matchin' pock-a-books would get everyone talkin'. You, the other half of me, are a genius! My famous hearts-and-stars sheets live on! Has Stacey seen yours yet? Tell me what she says . . . oh, and tell me if she is okay for our the-three-of-us-hang-out to be the weekend after *Grease* has its final curtain (must say I will kinda miss it but also not 'cuz I wasn't Sandy but the theater is my home base, so until the Winter Play I will be a little lost in the woods).

I thought a wicked ton about your "who-to-date" list, and I think you're right, you should definitely go for Diego Conoso. First of all, he is so hot. And such a good soccer player, and he doesn't have a tail anymore, and he's best friends with Justin, so I just totally picture our stretch limo for Prom bein' me and Christopher, you and Diego, Stacey and Justin, and Tzoug and Dube, maybe. Who knows, but a girl can dream, right?

Triple *L*,
Tar

Tar,

I know . . . Diego, right? I even thought he was so cute with his tail. Fingers crossed!

Stacey is great with the weekend after *Grease*! So excited for us all to hang out. She loves our hearts-and-stars purses. Her words: "Whimsical and really well sewn." Not bad, huh?

Triple *L*,
BB Minkey

Dear Tara,

I hope you had an awesome weekend! Was that party fun on Friday night? I didn't do much Friday night. Just went to get pizza with my parents and then went to Premiere Video and rented *Pump Up the Volume*. It was awesome. Have you seen that movie? I bet you'd like it a lot.

Then Saturday I got together with Joy. We went to the mall and walked around and practiced our lines. You know the fountain there, the one across from Jack's Joke Shop? Well, we ended up sitting there for a while, and I just went for it. I asked her if she wanted to be my girlfriend. She told me that she was really touched and that she would think about it. She said that she really likes me a lot but doesn't want anything to get in the way of us doing our best jobs in *Grease*. She went to Stagedoor Manor (that famous acting camp in Lochsheldrake, New York), and she learned there that the top performers are super focused and make sure that their first priority is the work. I get it.

She said we could still hook up and that after the musical is over she will give me an answer and that likely it will be a yes.

The reason I asked her out is because I thought about Season, Reason, Lifetime, and I have a feeling Joy will be Lifetime.

I've never been in love. I think I could be with Joy, but I don't even know what REAL LOVE would feel like. Like, how would I know if I was in REAL LOVE?

Because it's you, I can tell you that I was kinda sad that Joy said she had to think about it, but it's cool, I guess. Opening night is only a week and a half away, so it's not that long to wait.

I can't wait to see you at rehearsal later. Is that weird?

Matt

Dearest Matt,

Of course it's not weird that you're excited to see me later. We're very, veeeery close friends now, and that's what happens when you are close with someone. You get an excited feelin' when you think about 'em.

What's the opposite of joy, Matt? Pain. That's what Joy should have been named. She was named wrong, Matt! Shame on her parents.

How dare she tell you that she will get back to you. You put yourself on the line. You opened your heart. That bitch had the audacity to trash your heart that way? Oh my god, I am soooo friggin' mad right now. That devious little woman. Stealin' my lead parts, my perfume, and now breaking my kid brother's heart. Who in the hell does this lady think she is? I mean, seriously, Matt. And we all know that bitch went to Stagedoor Manor in Lochsheldrake, New York. She is such a bragger. Talk about conceited. Oh my god, that one could write a book called *Conceited: The Story of a Girl Who Thinks She Is the Greatest Thing in This Town Because Her Hair Is Curly and Long and She Can Sing Awesome.* How come everyone falls for her hogwarsh? I see right thru her,

Matt. Always have. Little Joy Becky Bern girl thinks she can just walk around my town and my hallways breakin' hearts and stealin' parts.

Take the perfume back, Matt. I'm serious. Ask her for the bottle of Anaïs Anaïs back. She doesn't deserve it. And if she's smart she will hand it over without a second thought. I am so sorry, sweetheart. You are too good for Joy.

You know what? I'd like to take you to Camel Lot tonight. I'm gonna have to blindfold you on the way there, but once we arrive I will take it off. You know what? I won't even blindfold you. You can know how to get there because I TRUST YOU. I KNOW YOU WILL NEVER BETRAY ME.

I'm gonna pick you up tonight at 8. Walk down to the bottom of your street. I can't pick you up at your house 'cuz what if Christopher saw? It would just be too confusin' for someone like him. He's not the brightest candle on the Carvel cake, if you know what I mean. Do you know what I mean, Cookie Puss?

Camel Lot. Me. You. Tonight.

GET THAT Anaïs Anaïs BACK FROM JOY ASAP.

4-Eva and a Day,

Tara

Dear My Matt,

If you are readin' this folded note, that means you got the vanilla envelope I left in your dressin' room. Enclosed in the envelope you should find this note (durrrrr, you're readin' it, so obviously you found it) and a mix-tape entitled Songs from Camel Lot, Volume One, October. I'm wicked proud of the mix I made you, Matt. But I'll get to that in a sec.

It's opening night, Matt!!!!!! This is your star turn, and don't you forget it. I am very, veeeery proud of you. You walked into this high school two months ago and you said, "South High, here I AM!!!" I admire that. Most Freshmen would never have even tried for a lead role, but you did. You did, Matt. 'Cuz you're special. You're not like the other guys in theater, and you're not like the other guys in this school. Come to think of it, Matt, you're not like anyone else in our town. Are you an alien, Young Man? J to the k.

I still dream of playin' Sandy, but I gotta be honest, Patty Simcox has kinda grown on me. Or I on her. I sorta understand Patty. The girl on the outside lookin' in.

Ahhhhhhhhhhhh, there is sooooooooooo much to say.

I know we pinky swore not to write each other notes after

that night at Camel Lot, but I couldn't help it, Matt. I just couldn't. Do you have a safe? I do. If you don't have a safe, get one, and then you can put all my notes in it and I will of course put all your notes to me in my safe. I thought of that last night, and I was like, "Tara, you idiot. You and Matt can write notes, you jerk, you just have to make sure they can never get into anyone else's hands." This dumb town, as we know, can be a very tricky place.

I wonder what the Winter Play is gonna be. I actually look forward to doin' a straight play because I feel like sinkin' my teeth into some serious drama. Know what I mean? Hey, maybe we will finally get that chance to play opposite each other. It's almost certain if you-know-who doesn't try and steal my part. I know, I know . . . we aren't talkin' about her until she makes her DECISION on whether or not to be your girlfriend, but I think we both know her "True Colors" (one of the songs I put on your mix-tape.)

You know how I told you I was gonna go out for Halloween? Well, I've changed my mind. Minds do change, even in this town. Nope. I'm just gonna stay at my house and hand out candy. I'm a Senior, for god's sake. I think my trick-or-treatin' days are in my rearview mirror. So, if you and your friends decide on my neighborhood, you know you can always knock on my door. We give out real-size candy bars. We're not rich at all, but Halloween means a lot to my mom.

Wow. I just realized that there are so many lasts in my life right now. Last opening night of a Fall Musical at South High. Last Halloween here. But with lasts also come firsts. And I'd say this is a first. This. Us. Me and You. Matt and Tara. The couple that could be. We could be a Supercouple, Matt. I know we could. I know I'm gettin' way ahead of myself. I'm with an all-star athlete, Christopher Caparelli, and you are in waiting for . . . well, you know who. UGHHHHHH . . . WHY IS LIFE SO VERY COMPLICATED???

Have you stopped thinkin' about our night at Camel Lot, Matt? I haven't. The look on your face when I pulled up into the back parking lot of Brophy Elementary School and told you, "This is it. This is Camel Lot." You were so cute. I know you thought Camel Lot was gonna be this far-off place, but it's not. Sometimes the best things in life are right in front of us. But you gotta agree that it's the best spot in town to stargaze. How do you know about all those constellations, Matt? I had glow-in-the-dark star stickers on my ceilin', too, but you know as much as an astronaut.

So, the mix-tape I made you is a musical stroll down the memory lane that will forever be our first night together in Camel Lot. (I was surprised you didn't ask me why I call it Camel Lot. I'll tell you one day. If you ask.)

The first song is "Crazy for You" by Madonna. Followed by "Eternal Flame" by the Bangles. You know what? I'm not gonna tell you the rest. I purposely didn't write the songs on the tape 'cuz I wanted it to be a surprise for you, and here I go revealin'. I'm gonna stop myself. Take a listen after openin' night. Do you have a Walkman? Put it in there, lie on your bed, and remember.

That kiss was life-changin' for me, Matt. And you do have very big lips. Like a girl. J to the . . .

What's to become of us? I know we haven't talked a lot since that night, but we've both had a lot on our plates. I think we can do this. You know what I mean? We can just consider it another thing that I help you out with . . . teachin' you stuff about how to make a girl feel good. It's not like we're in love with each other and NO ONE WILL EVER FIND OUT!

We're just friends. Really good friends who get each other. It's almost like the universe, the constellations, forced us together.

Okay, Danny Zuko . . . until we meet again (which better be soon) . . .

xoxo,

Tara   ·

P.S. Put this note in a safe.

P.P.S. Buy a safe.

Stef!

I was just walkin' down F Hall and I saw Stacey Simon wearing your hearts-and-stars pock-a-book!

I feel light-headed. Before I leap to conclusions, Q explain? Did you drop it and couldn't find it and she found it and was wearing it until she could find you and give it back?

Or is there more to this story?

Let me know as soon as humanly possible!

Love you (I think),
Tara

Dear Tara,

Joy said YES!!!!!!!!!!!!!!!!

It was right after the show. I came looking for you to tell you, but you were talking to Chris. By the way, awesome flowers he bought you.

Thanks for making me that mix-tape. I am definitely gonna check it out.

You're the best. Hey, maybe we can go to Uncle Chung's all together or something. Get some crab rangoon and stuff.

I will never forget Camel Lot. That was a crazy night.

I'm probably gonna go trick-or-treatin' in my neighborhood. Joy and I are gonna go as Daisy and her preppy boyfriend from *Mystic Pizza*.

Did you hear what the Winter Play is gonna be? *The Diary of Anne Frank*!!!!!!!! Holy shit!!!!!! What part do you want?

xoxo,

Matt (boyfriend of Joy Rebecca Bernstein!!!!!)

NOVEMBER 1991

Bloom,

I have an awesome safe. It's fireproof!!!!

I have to clear out a bunch of my New Kids on the Block puffy stickers, but then I can lend it to you. Did you hear I got a job at Fanny Farmer Candy Shop? I can get you free gummy bears and Sour Patch Kids. I think it's the best candy store in town, but some people are arrogant and only get their candy when they go into the city with their families.

You were so good in *Grease*! You should be a movie star! You already look like Keanu Reeves from the "Rush, Rush" video, and that combined with how talented you are equals so much!! So many people in our grade make fun of you for being in theater, but they're just jealous. They all watch TV and movies. Where do they think those actors come from? THE THEATER!! I read that Eric Stoltz was in a lot of plays. And Christian Slater!

I love earth science! Mr. Sudmeyer is such a nice teacher, don't you think? I think it's awesome that I share a lab table with you. I'm writing this as you dissect an earthworm. Oh my god, Joey McIntyre is single!!! I read it in *Tiger Beat*. He only lives, like, 30 minutes from here. Do you think I'd ever have a chance with him? I know a million girls want to marry him, but I love him for him. And his awesome voice. Do you still like New Kids on the Block or not really 'cuz we're at South High now? Either way, I still think you're a great actor, Bloom.

Thanks for telling Andy Mackamolen that he was a jerk for calling me Thunder Thighs. He is sooooo mean, and it's not like he's gorgeous like you and the New Kids and Eric Stoltz and Christian Slater.

I heard you and Joy Bernstein are a couple right now? That makes so much sense. You are both so talented and cute. I LOVE JOY'S HAIR! Oh my god, she looks like the girl from *Mystic Pizza* and *Satisfaction*. You guys make the perfect couple. Do you think I should be on stage crew for the Winter Play? I hope you get a lead part again.

Okay, gotta pass you this note now that you're done dissecting that poor worm.

Good luck,
Pammy Shapiro

P.S. Why do you need the safe?

Dear Pammy,

Thank you so much for lending me your safe. That is awesome of you.

I still think New Kids are alright. And I bet Joey McIntyre would like you a lot. You're funny and cool and nice.

Andy Mackamolen is such a JERK! He always makes fun of everyone. You don't have thunder thighs, Pam. You're tall! Why is being different such a big deal around here?!

Besides, don't listen to the mean people. I don't. I don't give a crap what anyone says about me. If I did, then I would be too afraid to go for my dreams. And if your dream is to meet Joey McIntyre, then you should go for your dream. So many people make fun of stuff 'cuz they're afraid.

Yeah, you should definitely try for stage crew. It's fun being involved in plays in any aspect.

You know I love gummy bears and Sour Patch Kids. Since first grade. Wow, we have gone to school together for a wicked long time.

Joy is amazing. I think we'll be together for all of high school, even when she graduates a year before me. And hopefully we will get married.

Ummmm, I just need the safe for some writing I'm doing. Thanks for lending me it.

Matt Bloom

Tara,

I know you listen to your answering machine messages religiously, so I'm fairly certain you have gotten all of mine. But just in case you didn't get any of the seven of them, I will tell you here what I said . . . on all seven of them.

Stacey was holding my hearts-and-stars purse for a total of, I don't know, one minute while I ran to the bathroom.

While she loves our matching purses, she does not want one. Not sure if that was your concern, but Stacey has her own style and never copies anyone else's. Not that she doesn't love what we made but she (A) just isn't the kind of person who does things that other people do and (B) has so much respect for our lifelong friendship and thinks it is, her words here, "beautiful that you and Tara have each other and reflect your friendship in your purses."

I hope everything is okay at your house. I'm assuming that is why you haven't gotten back to me and why you blew off our night with Stacey. Not that I want anything bad to be happening at your house, but I just hope you're not icing me out because Stacey was holding my purse.

I would appreciate a response. Thanks.

Muchly and Moreso,

Stef

Dear Tara,

I got a safe. So you can still write me notes. Why haven't you written me back? I wrote you, like, 10 notes or more. I know you got them.

Anyway, I got a safe. Please write me back. I miss my friendship with you. And why are you ignoring me in the hallways and around the music room? Actually, anywhere I see you, you walk the other way or pretend I'm not there.

You're my "big sister," so please talk to me.

You and Chris seem super happy these days. I mean, whenever I see you guys together by your locker or in the caf, you always jump into his arms and make out with him. When I walked by you guys the other day in F Hall, did you pull up your shirt or was I seeing things?

I hope you are well. I hope life is treating you great. Maybe I will see you at auditions for *Diary of Anne Frank*????????

I am still hopin' we can go to Uncle Chung's together . . . me, you, Chris, and Joy.

~~Ho~~

I mean, take care,

Sat. Cat. Matt.

Hello Rick, William, Mickey . . .
M . . . M . . . M-M-M . . . OH, right . . .
MATT,

I'm sorry, Kid. I am once again strugglin' with your name.
I'm tellin' you, your parents shoulda thought a little longer
about your name 'cuz it truly is very, veeeery complicated
to remember for popular, busy, half-of-a-Supercouple girls
like me.

Oh my god, Matt, I am soooooooooooo (a thousand o's)
sorry you feel ignored by me. I'm a SENIOR, Matt, so I have a
ton of stuff to tend to in the hallways. So, if I'm in the middle
of chitchattin' with my Senior girlfriends or hearin' a Friday-
night plan from another popular person or makin' out with
the greatest man this town has ever seen (CHRISTOPHER
CAPARELLI A.K.A. HOTTEST GUY IN THE GREATER
NEW ENGLAND AREA), then my sincerest apologies if you,
a Freshman, got your feelings hurt.

Safe? Why did you get a safe? Did you rob a diamond store,
Young Man? Don't tell me 'cuz my uncle's a cop and I will have
to report you. I am confused as to why you got a safe and why
you would be wastin' ink tellin' me about it. Do you have an

obsession with safes, Matt? Is this an inside joke or somethin'? I truly wish I understood.

I am SOOO good. Thanks for askin'. Oh my god, my life is so busy lately. I have plans round the clock with important people, and I have colleges to apply to. This woman is gettin' the hell outta this town and how. But I love it here, Matt. I'm no townie . . . but I have gotten so much from this place.

So, what is up and junk? Yes, I did get your notes. And thank you sooooo much for writin'. Did I read them? Well, I'm not at liberty to say.

Oh, so you saw my breasts the other day in F Hall? How random. I was showing them to the LOVE OF MY LIFE. I didn't even see you there. I would never have pulled up my shirt if I knew you were there. Ewwwwwww . . . I just got nauseous. You saw my naked body? Oh my god, I need to, like, pretend I didn't know that. Pretend, Tara. Pretend. K.

I'm psyched it's gonna snow soon 'cuz I love skiing. And makin' snowmen. And playin' in the snow. I'm old but NOT THAT OLD!!! Sure, I don't trick-or-treat anymore, Matt, but only average people who probably say "mint condition" dress up as *Mystic Pizza* couples and trick-or-treat.

I do lovvvvvve my winter time. What with the hot cocoa (mmmmmm, maybe Kev Brandolini will come home for Christmas break . . . I bet he's even more muscular and gorgeous now that he's in college), and I can't wait for that first snow. I am a girl who loves the first snow of the season. I cuddle up with my lover by a roarin' fireplace, and I talk of dreams and hopes. Then, when the streets are blanketed in snow and the town is hushed, I take my lover to Camel Lot, and let's just say magical things happen.

I should have blindfolded you!! If you ever, EVER tell anyone in this ludicrous town about Camel Lot I will be seriously pissed off, and you don't wanna see this girl mad. I am a very reserved girl, Matt, but when pushed to the edge, oh my god!!! Did you ever hear about the fight I got into with TaRitzah Rodriguez? It's pretty legendary. She was bein' a bitch to me for, like, three months in a row, always makin' fun of me and crap. Finally, I snapped. I took off my earrings, and I socked the bitch right in her ear. She got cauliflower ear, Matt, but I don't think it was because of me. I think she was a wrestler. Anyway, she was also pregnant at the time, but I just thought she was gainin' weight. What? Like I'm supposed to assume 7th-graders are with child? TaRitzah Rodriguez was a trashy girl from the other side of the tracks for sure. I would never punch a pregnant lady, but news alert: Don't get pregnant if you're not married, Matt.

What do you even want from me, Matt? Why are you writin' me all these notes now? Your folding has gotten very good, by the way. Hmmmm, wonder where you learned that from!

I have a ton of preparation to do for the *Diary of Anne Frank* auditions. What part do I want? Well, Anne Frank, of course. You can tell your wife, Joy Rebecca Bernstein, that this Irish Catholic girl will be hiding in the attic this time around. K, hon? I will land the coveted role of Anne Frank. Hey, if a proper bat mitzvahed girl can be Sandy in *Grease*, a girl who had her first orgasm in church can play Anne Frank.

Fine, Matt. You can write me back and I will read your note, but only, and I mean only, if you state quite clearly what it is you want from me.

I have a ridiculously full life, and I don't have the literal time to get into it with a Freshman. You are lucky, very lucky, I have responded this time.

Be well in all your future endeavors,
Tara Maureen Murphy a.k.a. soon to be Anne Frank

Hey Stefanie,

Ever heard of people being wicked busy? I had to buy two new sleeves of microcassettes for my answering machine because I've been getting soooo many messages as of late. I actually had the bright idea to make myself a Return Call Sheet and I put it on my corkboard. I swear you are next or the next after the next. It's a long sheet.

Honestly, Stefanie . . . how many times do I have to say thank you for that time years ago when I spent a few nights at your house because my parents were goin' through some stuff? My GOD! No, Stef . . . sorry to bum you out, but everything at my house is soooo great!

And as for missing the night with you and that girl Stacey . . . sorry, hon . . . it just wasn't my top priority. Getting the role of Anne Frank is.

Hope you and Stacey had fun even though I wasn't there. Was she so upset that I bailed? I will add her to my call sheet to say hello. I'm sure I have her number somewhere.

Best,
Tara

Dear Tara,

Thank you so much for writing me back. I appreciate it a lot. You asked me to state clearly why it is that I am writing you. Here goes nothin' . . .

I can't stop thinking about you. And that kiss. Our kiss. That night at Camel Lot when you kissed me.

I know you are in love with Chris. And I'm in love with Joy. But I guess I also have feelings for you. I've never met any girl like you, Tara.

I think you'd make a great Anne Frank.

Much love,
Matt Bloom

Dear Sweet Matthew,

Hi, my Matthew. It's me, Tara. I got your note, and I have to say I cried. And some of my tears fell onto your note, smudgin' your beautiful handwritin'. But that's the price you pay when your heart feels things.

I have hidden your note (much like Anne Frank hid her diary) in my safe. Who knew that my safe would become the keeper of notes from Matt Bloom? I certainly didn't expect this twist so late in my high school career. Mattttttttttttttttttttttttttt. Hi. Shhhhhhhh. (While you read the rest of this note I want you to imagine me sittin' backstage in my candy cane skirt, okay? My long hair is wet, and I am brushin' it with my awesome brush. You enter. Backstage left. And you approach me. I feel shy, so I try to not be attractive, but you won't allow for such nonsense. You say, "Keep brushin' your long hair." I tell you that I feel fatigued from so much brushin', so I hand you my brush. I think you are gonna keep brushin' my hair, but you don't. You throw my brush, and it smashes into bits and pieces against the wall, and then you hold me . . .) Shhhhhh . . .

Matt, I feel so old and mature but still a kid in so many ways.

I know that your feelin's for me are pure and hard core. How could they not be? I feel the same way about you. This is crazzzzzzzy.

Look, I've never done anything like this before, but I have watched *General Hospital*. There are ways for star-crossed lovers to sneak around town and ultimately, some day in the future, end up on the docks together and hop aboard a container ship headed for somewhere better.

I'm sorry I was ignoring you, Babe. I just was feeling sad and hurt by you, so I put up my defenses. I'm an Irish Catholic girl. We know how to stop all feeling and move about the day as if nothing ever happened. I will never, ever, ever do that to you again. Unless you leave me no other option, but I know you wouldn't do that.

Listen, if I get the iconic role of Anne Frank this week, I will pick you up at the bottom of your street and take you to Camel Lot.

This time you will learn why a back parkin' lot at Brophy Elementary School is called Camel Lot.

Big kisses, my guy,
Tara

P.S. Sniff this note. That's not Trésor, Mattttttttttttttttttttttt.

Dearest Soup,

I'm so happy we talked last night. Even though our call was wicked brief, it was just so great to hear your voice and to put everything to bed. And I can't tell you how good it felt to cross you off my Return Call Sheet. Your name was loomin' over my head for days. Literally . . . 'cuz my call sheet is on my corkboard, which is over my desk so it was over my head. (How mad are we still that they changed Edna's Edibles to Over Our Heads on *Facts of Life*?? So stupid of them.)

I woke up this morning anew. It's like the fog literally lifted from my eyes. I think I truly have Senioritis, and I'm serious that I might even go to my doctor to get a second opinion.

Why did no one warn us of the roller coaster that is our final year at South High? College applications, plays (for me, not you, but you have so many wonderful interests), my last cheering competition in Nashville in February, Prom (who even knows what life is going to be like then and also it will be 1992 by Prom, so that's just one year further away from our childhood), and so many other things!

Life used to be so simple, Stef, and I guess with all the newness I have lost a bit of my footing. I've never been so, well, so like . . . AHHHH . . . have I? You've known me forever. (Oh my god, I just had a flashback of us playin' Bedroom-A-Class in my room. 'Member? We would line up our Cabbage Patches and give them each a pencil and paper, and we would be the teachers. I was Ms. Bugg, you were Ms. Butler. Bedroom-A-Class. Theresa Louise and Michelle Elaine were star pupils!) Oh, my Steffed Animal! I'm sorry if I've been not me-ish.

Can we just literally start our Senior year over? Let's definitely do what you said and set a new date with me, you, and Stacey. I will white-out any obligations in my Month-At-A-Glance for that! Let's all just move on and grow up! My god. It's this town, I'm certain of it. Our town just brings up so much stuff for all of us. It's like if you took us all out of this town and put us in the city we would all love each other and just be chill 'cuz we were walkin' every-where and takin' the train and LIVING! When you're not LIVING it's hard to LIVE, you know. Do you know what I mean?

Underneath the extreme chaos of Senior year, my life is in a really good place right now. Only thing that was out of order was my friendship with you. And I take responsibility

for that. Qwe officially move on? Oo, I like Qwe (Can we) . . .
should we add it to our secret dictionary?

Love you more than life.

LIVES, LOVES, LAUGHS,

Me . . . Tara

T Bag—

What is up, Beautiful? I was getting pizza with Tzoug and Dube and I wished you were there, sitting next to me. Why? 'Cuz you're my girl, and I love when you sit next to me when I'm eating pizza.

Good luck with Anne Frank (and beans).

C.P.C.

Christopher!!!

Anne Frank (and beans)? How dare you make jokes about a girl hiding in an attic to escape the Nazis. Anne was a girl, much like me, who saw the best in her town but had to hide away from the evil people. Oh, how I long to be Anne Frank.

I'm wearin' a wig at my audition tomorrow. It's brown and like shoulder length. I know, a wicked far cry from my long blond tresses but hey, an actress of my caliber transforms for proper roles.

And how are you, Mr. Mister? If my eyes weren't deceivin' me I coulda sworn I saw Kathy Connery squeezin' your ass after homeroom. True or false?

Sluts like Kathy have no boundaries, Chris. Don't get me wrong, I adore Kath and we have tons of history, but she is a slut and she loves a good hockey ass, which you have. So . . . spill the beans, and don't say "Anne Frank" just 'cuz I said "beans."

xoxoxoxoxoxoxo,

Anne Frank Maureen Murphy

T,

You caught us. Yeah, Kathy grabbed my ass. She said she was squeezin' all the Varsity Hockey bums to make an educated ASS-essment of whose was the best. I won!!!! You know Kathy. She loves to flirt. She's harmless. I'd never touch her anyway . . . why? 'Cuz I got you.

C.P.C.

Hello my co-star,

Matt! Today has got to be the greatest day of my life! God dammit, I'm ANNE FRIGGIN' FRANK!

What a shame that Joy Rebecca Bernstein opted out of auditions. I was hopin' for some competition, but maybe she just got worried that I had the part locked. Joy would be a good Anne Frank if this were a junior high production, but it's the big leagues. And to think, you are playin' the sweet role of Peter. Anne's love interest. So many things can happen in a stuffy attic, Matt. So many private things. Q believe we have two whole months together? I am simply overcome with happiness.

And because I got the lead role, as promised I'm gonna pick you up at the bottom of your street and take you to Camel Lot. Oh, Matt, our future is bright.

Always,
Your Anne Frank

P.S. Not that I care, but why did Joy not audition? Seems very unlike her.

Tara,

Congratulations!!!! I am so happy for you. And for us. We are gonna have the best time doing this play together.

You didn't hear about Joy? Oh. I thought everyone knew. She couldn't audition for *The Diary of Anne Frank* because she got the role of Eponine in a regional production of *Les Misérables*. She starts rehearsals today, actually. I guess some *Les Miz* scouts came to our production of *Grease* and were blown away by Joy as Sandy, so they offered her Eponine. Offered!!!!! She didn't even have to audition. There's talk of her moving to the Broadway production after her run ends. Crazy . . .

I will meet you at the bottom of my street tonight. What time?

Your Matt

Oh, hey Matt,

Yeah, tonight's not gonna be good anymore to go to Camel Lot. I forgot I have to hang out with Christopher. He is my boyfriend, so I guess he is priority.

Joy is playing Eponine in *Les Misérables*? You do know that that is my number-one dream role of all time, right? Was this a master plan, Matt? Did you encourage this? I literally can't even believe this, Matt. I am heartbroken right now. You heard me sing "On My Own" at *Grease* auditions. You know how good I am at it. I HATE THIS TOWN!!!!!

How is this girl living out my entire life? How is this happening? I feel light-headed.

It's okay. It's totally okay. I'm Anne Frank, and that's all that matters.

Cheers,
Tara

YAY!

I am beyond thrilled for you, Tara!! Anne Frank! What an achievement. You are going to get into any college you want now! What school would pass up such a multitalented girl? And all your extracurriculars! You basically started the Thanksgiving Turkey Drive. Do you know how many needy families have had a happy Thanksgiving because of you? I can't wait to do the drive with you again. Oh my god, it's so soon.

Yes, yes, yes, we are totally moved on! I love QWE, by the way. Believe me, I know how insane this year is. We are all overwhelmed. You know I love my parents more than anything, but they are pushing me so hard to get into Northwestern because they both went there. It's a wonderful school, but what if I don't get in? Are they going to disown me?

We are on with Stacey for next Saturday! Excited for you two to finally get to know each other, and you know what? Our world is expanding, Tara. That's pretty cool . . . a lovely precursor to what college will be like, right?

Love you, BB Minkey, and SO BEYOND HAPPY FOR YOU!

xoxoxxoxo,

Soup

Soup!

How incredible was our hangout with Stacey?! I will happily answer that: BEYOND INCREDIBLE!! The three of us make so much sense together! All of us are smart and kind, wicked well-dressed, and pretty. It's just sooo rare that three girls who check off all those boxes find each other, ya know? Stacey is just so great. That was so funny when she told us how her hair got mangled in her cotillion dress zipper! I didn't even know that. Did you?? And how her mom had to use olive oil to get it out, which ruined her dress but she didn't care because she just threw on somethin' else and her jean jacket and was like, "This'll be fine." Hey, if anyone knows the painful struggles of havin' wicked long hair, it's this girl. Us longer-haired girls go through a lot, but it's definitely worth it. If you ever grow yours out, you will sooo get it, Steffed Animal.

It was just an all-around solid night, Stef. Loved talkin' about colleges with her, and I really do get why she wants to go to school in Vermont . . . I've always seen her earthy-crunchy side. I'm sure she's like, "Once I get outta this judgmental town I can finally wear my Birkenstocks!" No one gets us here, but that's okay . . . University is just around the bend. Don't you think it was cute how Stacey was like, "Tara, when you get into NYU, and Stef, when you get into Northwestern, and when I get in to my school in Vermont . . . let's all go to dinner to celebrate!!" So adorable. I wonder where we'll go to dinner? In the city, definitely, don't you think?

Anyway . . . what an awesome night.

Love you SO MUCH,
Tara

P.S. Which college is she hopin' to go to in Vermont? You don't know, do you? Not that it matters.

Tar,

Wasn't that a fabulous night? I am so happy it FINALLY happened, and I just knew that if you got to spend quality time with Stacey you would see how lovely she is. I had a feeling you would get that she isn't at all what you thought she was. I am so happy you guys know each other now. SO HAPPY!! Yay!

Oh and I have no idea where in Vermont Stacey is planning on going to college. She is so private about that, which I totally respect.

Lives, Loves, Laughs . . .
Stef

Tara—

You okay? I'm really sorry that they canceled *The Diary of Anne Frank*. You would have been awesome in it. You can always perform it for me in my bedroom. My mom's goin' out of town, so we can pretend my house is the attic and I'm a bad guy tryin' to find you but when I see how beautiful you are I have second thoughts. Then we hook up. Love you. You're awesome. Hey, you always have your cheerleading competition to focus on. You will definitely win Nationals this year.

Love ya,

C.P.C.

To-est my sweet Tara—

Oh my god, I just heard! Are you okay? I do not know
what to say except I love you and I am always here for you.

Love,
Stef

Dear Tara,

Hey. I'm not really sure what to say. I can't believe they canceled the Winter Play. I heard it's because musicals draw a much bigger audience, so the ticket sales are higher, which earns more money for the theater department. But it's great news that there will still be a Spring Musical. I wonder what it will be?

I know you are really upset right now, Tara. I was really excited to play opposite you in *The Diary of Anne Frank*. I have no doubt that you would have been incredible as Anne. But I bet you will get a lead role in the Spring Musical. I know you want one more lead role before you graduate. That means a lot to you. I know it does. Man, I am bummed for me, but I am more bummed for you about this. Are you okay?

Thinkin' about you,
Matt

Hey Matt,

I appreciate you checkin' in on me. I can't really put into words how I feel right now.

Maybe I just don't deserve good things? Maybe I was cursed or something. Do you know what I mean?

I feel so connected to Anne Frank. Now more than ever. Both of us awesome girls, being punished just for bein' who we are. I know that one day I will play Anne Frank and chances are it will be on Broadway.

I am writing this note to you, Matt, as I watch the first snowflakes fall to the ground. Here I thought I would be spending the first snowfall of the season in the arms of someone who loves me, but I gotta admit, I think it's best if I just spend it alone, in my bedroom.

I think that I'm gonna take the rest of November for myself. I've been giving so much of myself to others lately it feels like I forgot about me. I will continue to be Christopher's girlfriend, but I am gonna limit the time I spend with him. And as for you and me, well, Matt, I think it's best for us to chill out. I can't be your girl on the side. Joy is your priority, and I'm your afterthought. I can no longer come in second place. No sir.

I care deeply for you, Matt. But let's be honest. You're gonna lose your virginity to Joy. As these snowflakes fall from the clouds up above, I can't help but think about LOVE. What would it be like to be truly loved by a Freshman boy? To feel the big lips of a handsome young star pressed against mine? I imagine a world where this young star tells me he loves me and then asks me to take his virginity from him, thus tying us together 4-eva. Gosh, if that could happen I probably wouldn't feel sad about not playin' Anne Frank. But who might this handsome star Freshman be? Does he exist or only in my mind's eye? Could he love me the way I long to be loved?

Oh, Matt. There's gotta be an inch of snow on the ground now. Enough to make a snowman. I might have to go gather my mittens and parka and head on out into the great white open. I bet if you were here with me we would throw snowballs at each other and laugh, then sit by a roarin' fire and talk about what's to come. And maybe, just maybe, we would, well . . .

Be well, Cuteheart. And know that I will be fine. I'm just a girl on a snowy night in a town where some dreams get crushed . . . and some dreams come true . . .

My heart belongs to?????????????????
Tara M. Murphy

P.S. I am gonna fold this note really tight and put it in your earth science lab table tomorrow. Durrrr, you already know that if you're reading this.

Hey Tricia,

Oh my god, you have to pinky swear that you will not tell anyone what I'm about to tell you, oh my god, you are gonna freak out. Okay, so you know how I share a lab table with Matt Bloom? Well, I, like, reached into my desk to grab my textbook and there was a super tight folded note, so I, like, opened it, of course, because it was in my side of the desk, and oh my god, it wasn't for me—it was for Bloom!!

The note was from Tara Murphy. You know the Senior girl who goes out with the hockey player, Chris Caparelli? She is in a lot of the plays and is a cheerleader! You know her. She's kind of popular and always wears short skirts. The girl with long blond hair. Okay, I know you know who she is. Anyway, she wrote Bloom this note and, um, PROMISE YOU WON'T SAY A WORD TO ANYONE because I like Bloom and he's such a good actor, but holy shit!!! Bloom and Tara are basically having an affair. But in the note Tara sort of told him that she is done with him because he is going out with Joy Bernstein and she doesn't want to be the woman on the side. Wowza!!!

I never pegged Bloom for someone who would cheat on his girlfriend. And from the sound of the note it seems like Bloom is the one trying to get Tara to hook up.

Maybe I can get more information. Oh my god, oh my god!!! This is like *Tiger Beat*. I love South High!

Are you stopping by Fanny Farmer Candy Shop this weekend? We have a special on pounds of gummy worms.

Pammy

P.S. PINKY SWEAR you won't tell anyone.

Pammy,

Holy ballsack! I know you love Matt Bloom, but he's not all he thinks he's cracked up to be. Yeah, he looks like Keanu Reeves from the "Rush, Rush" video, but who gives a crap . . . Kid is so full of himself, he walks around like he owns this school and thinks he's above everyone and come on . . . he's a friggin' theater geek. Whatever, I know you love theater geeks.

Tara Murphy is kind of a slut though, right? She went out with Timmy Garabino, and my sister Jenny was so pissed off about that she and Megan Dooley t.p.'d her mailbox. Rightfully so . . . everyone knew my sister and Timmy had hooked up back in middle school. And she used Kev Brandolini so she could hang out in his mansion and ride his horses. Well, that's what Jenny and Megan told me, and they should know.

I won't tell anyone, Shapiro. Calm down.

Love ya and yeah, I'll swing by Fanny Farmer Candy Shop while I'm at the mall this weekend. I've got a mint condition turtleneck on layaway at Marshalls, so I'll pick that up then come by.

Later, Khed,
Tricia

Deena,

Hey, girl. Okay, you know my tall friend Pam Shapiro who I went to Callahan Middle with? She told me some crazy shit. But you can't say anything.

Okay, do you know who Matt Bloom is? He went to Callahan Middle, too, so you might not know who he is. Anyway . . . he's in our grade and he's kinda hot . . . he looks kinda like Keanu Reeves, but he's not Keanu but he thinks he is? Wicked conceited kid. Well, apparently he is sleeping with Tara Murphy. Chris Caparelli doesn't know about it yet, and I guess Bloom is the one who instigated the whole affair. And to make shit more outta control, Bloom's girlfriend, Joy, that Sophomore with the awesome curly hair, is in the city all the time 'cuz she is in some weird musical *Lay Mizarob* or something, so she doesn't even know anything that's happening here!

Crazy, right? Meet me in the parking lot later and we'll smoke some butts and discuss. I wanna get plastered this weekend, by the by.

Love you, Khed,
Tricia

Pete,

What's up, you friggin' tool? Yo, I got some serious news for you, buddy.

David Bloom's younger brother, Matt, is drilling Tara Murphy. Behind your boy Caparelli's back! How messed up is that?

They've been bangin' since the beginning of the year, and Bloom is trying to force Murphy to keep the affair going, but I guess she is trying to shut it down.

Whatever. What's up with you, you friggin' douchebag?!! Wanna hook up?

Anyway, I'll be smokin' butts with Tricia in the parking lot later, so come by, you filthy pig.

Love ya, Khed,
Deena

Yo C.P.C.,

Hey, bro. I am sorry to be the one to tell you this, but you're my boy, so I feel like I should.

That Freshman kid who lives in your neighborhood, Matt Bloom, well, I think he's been taking advantage of sweet Tara.

I don't really know the details, only what I've heard, but it sounds pretty messed up, dude.

Sorry to be the one to tell you, Khed.

Pete

Dear Tara,

Before I confront Matty B., I need to cross-reference some things I've been hearing today. I'm pretty mad right now, but I will write this as good as I can.

Are you sleeping with Matt?

Pete wrote me and then I went to talk to him, and this is what I know. Pete found out from Deena, who found out from Tricia, who found out from some girl named Pammy Shapiro, whoever the fuck that is. This Shapiro chick supposedly found a note from you to Matt in her desk.

Tara? What should I make of this?

Write me back as fast as you can 'cuz right now I want to beat the shit out of Matt.

Chris

Dearest Christopher Patrick Caparelli,

You know I only use your middle name when things are on high alert, and I would say that this is the highest alert our Supercoupledom has ever seen.

Let me first address some of the names you referenced in your note to me.

Your friend Pete Hickey is a skid. You know that, I know that. The whole friggin' town knows that. He works at his cousin's gas station, Chris. Proper jobs for high school people are landscapers or lifeguards. Pete is a dirtbag times ten. The furthest he will ever get from this town is the next town over. I have been telling you since we started dating that boys like Tzoug and Dube are guys like you. Good guys. Guys who will do somethin' with their lives. But Pete? Puhhhlease. His nipple is pierced, Chris. I mean, come on! He has a tattoo of a friggin' shamrock next to his balls. I'm more Irish than the queen of Ireland, but do you see me rockin' a friggin' shamrock tattoo? No.

So, trustworthy, dependable Pete Hickey gave you this news, huh? If I'm not mistaken, the last time Pete gave you news it was that he "accidentally" drove through your garage door because there was "black ice" on your driveway. IT WAS MID-SPRING, Chris!!!!!!

Sit back, hon. I'm just gettin' started. You write me a note with accusations like I'm some townie whore, and guess what, you will get a note like this. I think by the end of this one I will be the one needing to make some decisions, Caparelli!!

So, Pete Hickey heard from Deena DeLuca a.k.a. Skunk Bush. Know why her nickname is Skunk Bush, Chris? Because good, sweet, pure, innocent Deena DeLuca was hookin' up with some guys in front of the pond at Flanagan State Park. And lo and behold, as it happens sometimes in parks, a skunk strolled by and sprayed Deena right between her legs. SKUNK BUSH! Deena has been beating girls up since first grade. She is a wicked witch. She eggs houses and shaving creams cars. She trips people in hallways (I've never done that and Stef knows it, and what happens between me and my best friend is none of your friggin' business anyway) and stirs up trouble all around this town. She is as evil as a girl can be, and you actually referenced that vile creature in a folded note to me!!!!!! SUGGESTION!!: Never ever write the name Deena DeLuca in a note to this girl. I don't share college-ruled paper with trash like that.

You comfortable, Caparelli? 'Cuz I'm literally just warming up.

Tricia "Trish" Simms. Well, I guess the kindest thing one could say about Tricia is that she isn't the dumbest person in this town. Her sister Jenny is. Those Simms sisters have been gunnin' for me since as far back as I can remember. I'm sorry you're 4'11" on the hoof, Trish, but that's not my goddamn problem! Don't hate me 'cuz I'm 5'6" and a half. That little weeble wobble can't even go on roller coasters, and she's mean!! In what friggin' world does a pint-sized grown woman get away with being mean? I'll tell you what world, Caparelli . . . THIS ONE!!!! The rules of the real world do not exist here. In the real world, little munchkins aren't popular . . . they're sold by the dozen at Dunkin' Donuts!!! I AM ON FIRE, CAPARELLI!!!!! ON FIRE!!!!

And this all started from Pamela Pammy Pam Shapiro. You know, it's a real shame that Pam caused this shit storm because I have seen her in the hallways (how can you not—she's a friggin' giant), and I have had nothing but kind thoughts for her. But, as they say in America, the gloves are off. That linebacker has another thing comin' to her thinkin' she can start a rumor so vicious it got us here. Not surprising that Pammy Shapiro would start this as she must not have anything in her own life to be excited about except for thinkin' she's gonna marry Joey McIntyre one day. And stop callin' yourself Pammy, that's an adorable littler girl's name. You're not adorable, and you're far from bein' a littler, so . . . Pam'll do just fine.

Are you pickin' up what I'm puttin' down? Are the pieces of this wild puzzle coming together for you, Chris?

We live in a town filled with people who are obsessed with other people. And this high school is ground zero.

And about the note. The note that was in PAM Shapiro's desk. Let me say first that I am just surprised that lady didn't eat my note thinkin' it was a Stella D'oro snack cookie or somethin'. But alas, she didn't eat it. She read it.

I am not going to defend that note, Christopher. The note was real, Kid. It was written and delivered. The note happened. But let's take a minute here to fully understand the content of the note and the timeline said note was written and delivered.

I had just landed the role of a lifetime. Anne Frank. Then that play was canceled by what has to be the most idiotic school board in the history of public schools. I lost my role and was subsequently devastated. In my devastation I, still channeling Anne Frank (who was a famous writer that wrote descriptive notes to others and herself), wrote a note to Matt Bloom . . . YOUR ACROSS-THE-STREET NEIGHBOR THAT YOU INTRODUCED ME TO AND BEGGED ME TO BE KIND TO!!!! Remember that, Caparelli?

Yes. I wrote Matt Bloom a long-winded note as if I were Anne Frank. I can't even remember what the note said because I was ANNE FRANK when I wrote it, and, well, she's dead, so we can't exactly ask her now, can we???!!!!!!

I wrote a character note to another actor. Oh, sorry, let me write that again in a language you'll understand . . . I, uh, like, ummmmm, wrote a, ummmm, note pretendin' I was, uhhhh, someone else to another, ummmm, ACTOR!!

This is interesting, though. Pretty revealin', too. I delivered a note to the wrong side of a science lab table and who finds it but a portly Freshman giant.

The giant tells a munchkin. The munchkin tells Skunk Bush. Skunk Bush tells the king of all skids. The king of all skids tells you, and YOU BELIEVE ALL OF THEM!! You took the word of a pathetic Greek chorus of delinquents! I think that raises some questions, Chris. I think that raises a lot of questions. You should take a look at that, you know, for you and your own growth.

Interesting this all happened right before Thanksgiving break. Key word. BREAK!!!! Something I think we need.

There. I left it all on the dance floor. Ahhhhhhh, dance floors. Proms. The Senior Prom that will be held in the big city this spring. Our last hoorah as Seniors, as citizens of this town. Will we be going as the Supercouple we were? Will we dance to "I've Had the Time of My Life"? I can't say for sure.

Fall of 1992 can't come fast enough. College, can you hear me? Broadway? Hey, it's me, Tara Maureen Murphy . . . I will see you soon. As if bein' stripped of Anne Frank wasn't hurtful enough. The love of my life goes and basically subpoenas me to the court of jealous townies.

Consider this my last folded note to you, Christopher. Until, of course, the tides turn.

Oh, look at that . . . it's snowin' outside. The high school parkin' lot is turnin' white before my very eyes, and here I am, hidin' under a stairwell, penning this here note to a person I thought I could trust.

Tara

P.S. Tonight I will make a mix-tape with some of the following songs. Wonder if you can guess the theme I'm goin' for.

1. On My Own (from *Les Misérables*)
2. Fast Car
3. Time for Me to Fly
4. Every Rose Has Its Thorn
5. The Breakup Song
6. Don't You (Forget about Me)

Hey Tara,

I'm gutted right now. Is this true about you and Chris's across-the-street neighbor? You know I'm not one to believe gossip, but I just can't help but think this might be true. It just adds up. Is this why this year has been so rocky for us? I can't help but think maybe it is.

Look, not to be rude, but you've always been a little, well, vibrant. But that makes sense, you're incredibly talented! And besides that I have always just loved you for you. Best friends accept each other, warts and all. But best friends also share honestly with each other.

I don't care if what people are saying is true or not true or half-true or whatever. I care about you telling me because, Tara, I'm not sure I know how to be a friend to someone, let alone a best friend to someone, who isn't being authentic.

Please write me back before the Turkey Drive. I really don't want to be there, wrapping turkeys with you, if we haven't cleared the "polluted, storm-cloud-filled" air.

Thanks much,
Stefanie

Dear Tara,

I believe you!

I'm so sorry I even suggested this stupid rumor might be true. Of course you wrote a character note to Matty B. You're a friggin' artist. That's why I love you. And why I love the love we make. Together.

How could I think that my little buddy Matty B. would even think about moving in on you? He's the best little guy I know.

And you're right about those "friends" of mine. I've just known some of them for so long, and you know how loyal I am. But I am gonna call Pete and Deena and tell them to back off and stop spreading this bullshit. I will tell them to deal with those losers Tricia Simms and Pam whatever-the-hell-her-name-is.

Please, Tara. Please don't take a break. I know that if you ever heard a stupid rumor about me doing anything with some other girl you would never believe it, so what a dick I am for believing this bullshit.

I'm a tool.

You're hotter than ever.

You're the sweetest person I know.

I love you, your fragrance, and your body.

C.P.C.

Dear "Thanks Much,"

Hey there, Stefanie. How are you? As you can see, I have photocopied Christopher's apology note so you can read for yourself the goings-on of a November in the life of Tara Maureen Murphy. Wow, this school just loves a good Tara rumor, huh? Who woulda thunk that you, too, would be titillated enough to get in on this, Stefanie.

Nah, Stef, the me and Matt Bloom stuff isn't true. Sorry, hon. I know, what a snooze-fest I am, huh? I guess my real-life drama isn't enough to satiate the needs of some townspeople who can't seem to find their own lives interesting enough. Nope, they gotta feed off mine and manufacture even more about me.

I wish there was a pill I could take that would just knock me out until I woke up in my NYU dorm room with my fabulous (your favorite word) roommate. I wonder what she will be like. I bet her name is gonna be Victoria. I can call her Tori. We will be Tori and Tara, and we will be best friends, mark my words. Tori will be regal. She will hail from a phenomenal family. Maybe she's a Kennedy. Yup. Victoria Kennedy. And she has a house, no . . . a compound ON ISLAND. But not

Nantucket. Eww. Martha's Vineyard!! And Tori always takes me to her compound ON ISLAND. She even christens one of the guesthouses as "Tara's Bungalow." We go sailing and buy matching handwoven pock-a-books. We swim a ton and just lollygag around ISLAND on most days. Our dinners are long and filled with laughter and intelligent, well-traveled, very, veeerry cultured conversation. Chef makes the most divine lobster bisque. Have you tried it? No, 'cuz you're not there!

Oh my GOD, Stef! You went away for one little summer and you came back so different. It's like life recast you in the role of yourself.

Maybe I am having a hard-to-explain relationship with Matt Bloom. Maybe I don't understand what this Freshman idiot has done to my brain. But how could I even trust telling you the deepest, most real parts of me now that you are so close with Stacey Simon?

"Oh, there Tara goes again freaking out about Stacey Simon."

"Why can't Tara just go with the flow? I mean, she had a great hangout with Stacey Simon, and it was wicked obvious Stacey Simon thought Tara was incredible on so many levels, so hasn't Tara seen for herself that Stacey Simon isn't all that bad?"

Stef, isn't she THAT BAD? It took you running her over for her to say one word to you. Years and years in the same town, at the same schools, and not ONE WORD, but you run her over and suddenly she speaks? And I guess only ON ISLAND can my lifelong best friend run over a declared enemy and become her confidante.

Yes, I'm upset right now! Why couldn't your note to me have been:

"Dear Tara, these horrible people. Making up crap about you. Losers. Lowlifes."

Nope, it had to be you not believing in me!!

I think I can forgive you if you come to the Turkey Drive. K?

Hearts and Stars,

Tara

Tara,

Sorry I upset you. You're right . . . I should have just had your back completely. And you know you can tell me anything and everything, Tara. This Matt kid is really annoying you, huh? That's the last thing you need right now in your life. My advice: Just steer clear of him.

I will absolutely be at the Turkey Drive!

xoxo,

Stef

Dear Matt,

Listen, as you know, a lot has transpired in the last 24 hours. I am very sorry that I put that note on the wrong side of your science lab table. Do you hate me?

I will never put a note in your lab table again. What a slip-up on my end. I usually cross my t's and dot the heck out of my i's, but every romantic has their day in court, do you know what I mean?

What an evil heavier girl that <u>PAM</u> Shapiro is. And here I was praying for her to have an easy time at South High, what with her height and width. Sometimes prayers are said for the wrong people, Matt. I know that now.

As you can see, I will only sneak notes into your locker from here on out or until another, better location pops into mind. I could leave them in your mailbox at your house, but would your mom find 'em? Is she nosy? My mom is. My mom stole my candy cane skirt the other day and wore it around the house. Thank GODDDDDDDDD I am nothin' like her and so much like my dad 'cuz he's got his shit together.

I am thankful that you, unlike most of the people in this messed-up town, keep your word. You didn't say anything to anyone about the location of Camel Lot. That's sooooo good, eXpecially now, Matt. 'Cuz as it stands, Camel Lot is gonna be our only refuge. Our safe harbor. Our docks . . .

After the Thanksgiving dinner I am gonna wait at the bottom of your street. I will wait from 8 to 8:30, and if you come to meet me I promise to take you to Camel Lot and tell you why I named it that.

Is everything smoothed over with you and Joy? Did she hear about the "rumor"?

Christopher had the audacity to accuse me of having a sexual relationship with you. Q even believe? You're losin' your virginity to Joy. I'm no fool. But don't worry, Matt. I didn't tell him anything. Not about the kiss or anything. It's not my fault I have feelings for you. If it's anyone's fault it's your mom and dad's . . . 'cuz they created you. Maybe I should yell at them. J to the k, Matt.

I feel bad about Christopher but . . . He's so many things, but you he is not. I could work wicked hard to make it work with him (the way my parents have with each other for, like, a billion years), but what life is that? Is that my destiny?

Oh, I pray it snows when I pick you up after Thanksgiving dinner at the bottom of your street.

We need to go to Camel Lot together to escape the chaos, Matt.

Again, I am sorry for my terrible mistake.

Your "friend,"
Tara

Dear My On-a-Break Boyfriend,

I have received your apology note, and I admire you for it.

I appreciate that you are speaking to your lesser-than "friends" and telling them to back off. Thanks.

Is it okay with you that I've become buddies with Matt Bloom? Or did you want me to be nice to him and hate him? I'm confused, Christopher.

I will take your note into consideration. I still love you very much, but this whole event has really made me take pause.

So, I ask for your patience as I take stock of my life. Can you give me that, Mr. Accusation?

Look, do I miss bein' naked with you? Yeah. Do I miss dancin' around your room in your hockey jersey? Yep. Why do I miss those things? Hmmmmmmmmmm . . . BECAUSE I LOVE YOU.

But my heart is real, Christopher. It's a beating, pulsing thing, and you broke a piece of it. So it needs to mend. And unlike my Cabbage Patch Kid, Theresa Louise (who broke her braid six years ago and I took her to the Cabbage Patch Kid Hospital), there is no hospital for a broken teenage heart.

Respectfully yours,

T

Tara,

Time is all I got, baby girl. I will wait for you as long as you
need. How long do you think? No pressure. But how long??
  I'm horny.

Love ya,
C.P.C.

Hey Kath,

We're all set. Tara is definitely not coming over during Thanksgiving break, so we are on like Donkey Kong.

You can live out all your Varsity Hockey–player fantasies . . . wear my jersey, put on my skates, etc., etc., etc. . . .

Can't wait to see you.

Signed, Best Hockey Butt in New England . . .

Chris Caparelli

DECEMBER 1991

Dear Kathy—

Hey, girl! How are you, and what are you up to these days? How was your Thanksgivin'? Do anything special??

I just wanted to write to say that your skin looks amazin'! Whatever product you're usin' should win an award because, oh my god, you look like a different person! I would ask you what the product is but I've never had skin issues. I know, insane, right? Like, not even one zit. I probably just jinxed myself!! But seriously I always wanted braces, but unfortunately the orthodontist refused me every time I went in 'cuz he was like, "Tara, you have perfect teeth." So I did the paper-clip, tin-foil thing and pretended I had braces. Same thing with my skin. No one knows this (but you and I go way back), but I bought Oxy Pads with benzoyl peroxide at Medi Mart just to use them even though I had literally nothing on my face to clear up. I know . . . I'm so quirky. But your face, Kathy . . . flawless now! (Don't walk into a modeling agency unless you are prepared to sign the contracts, ya know?!)

Oh my god . . . I heard you're not even applyin' to colleges 'cuz you're just gonna stay workin' at Coconuts. I bet you'll be manager there in no time 'cuz you're sooo good at retail. So jealous of people like you. Would I trade bein' incredibly talented for bein' amazin' at retail? I'd honestly have to think about that one, Kath.

Do you get wicked good discounts on CDs? I bet it's awesome to work at a music store. I mean, for me it would be, as I am a huge fan of music. But I'm sure you know that as everyone knows that about me. Yep, that's always me blastin' songs in my Wagoneer (tee-hee, tee-hee). I am obsessed with "Rush, Rush" right now. And that video with Keanu Reeves!!! Come on! If I met a guy who looked like Keanu Reeves I would dump Christopher in one second. Not that a Keanu Reeves–lookin' guy would ever be anywhere close to our town, but just sayin'. But you know how much I love Christopher (MORE THAN LIFE), so I guess it's a win-win for everyone that there are no Keanus around this tri-state area.

Anyway, Old Glowing-Skinned Friend, when I'm at University and you're manager at Coconuts (or OWNER—who knows, right?) we will always be able to look back at that time in life when we were kids and teenagers together, growin' up, makin' mistakes, learnin', fumblin', tumblin', livin'!

Can you believe 1991 is crawlin' to a close? You know what, Kathy? Maybe we should hang out? I would LOVE to hang out with you! Am I super busy? YES! Am I gonna start trainin' for Nashville? You betcha! Is Stef still, all these years later, my number one priority? Better believe it! Did I recently become friends with Stacey Simon? Crazier things have never happened, but that answer would be YES! And am I one half of a very solid Supercouple? Yep. Yar, I am, Kath! Even foolish middle-school-level rumors can't break the iconic bond me and Christopher Caparelli have!

Let's do it. Let's hang out me and you! We are gettin' a stretch from Kurt Cutter's dad's limo company for Prom, so I bet we would have room in there for you and who? WE NEED TO GET YOU A BOYFRIEND, YOU ARE SO BEAUTIFUL, <u>NOW</u>! By Prom time Stef will (fingers crossed) be fully goin' out with someone amazing (can't say who because it's between us best friends and Stacey Simon), and you deserve someone awesome, too. I know you've always loved bein' single and just hookin' up, but college (and not college) is around the corner, Kath. Good time to change things up, right?

Consider this note a super kind gesture, and I mean it when I say let's get you a boyfriend. K, girl?

W/B/S

Tara Murphy (likely Caparelli in the future)

Pam—

While I appreciate all the bags of gummy worms and sour cherries you continue to leave on my desks in every classroom, near my bag, and taped to my locker, I am going to be really honest with you. Please stop. I don't want your candy. And please take your safe back. I keep giving it to you and you keep putting it in my backpack when I'm not looking. Stop that. I don't want your candy, Pam, and I don't want your safe! In fact, I don't want anything from you. So you're not surprised, I have asked for my lab table to be changed. Tomorrow, we will no longer share a desk. And if I have it my way, Pam, we will never again share a desk at South High.

I understand that you found a note on your side of our lab table. I don't really understand you opening that note and reading it because it said "TO MATT" on it. I thought, when you gave it to me, that you were exactly the Pammy Shapiro I've always been friends with. The Pammy Shapiro I've always seen the best in. The Pammy Shapiro I loved and the Pammy Shapiro I truly believed could one day marry Joey McIntyre. But now . . . now I don't think Joey Mac would like you because I bet a guy like him doesn't like betrayers like you, Pam!

When you got stuck in the Lemon Squeeze at Macomber Day Camp, who told everyone to stop laughing and pointing? Me! Who ran and got a counselor to help you? Me! Who helped that counselor get you out of the Lemon Squeeze? I did, Pam. I can't believe that camp lets kids walk through a crack in a boulder but they did, and you got stuck and I got you out.

And then there was the time we were playing four square and that asshole Andy Mackamolen threw the ball so hard in your face you got the wind knocked out of you and fell and broke your wrist. I was so mad I pushed Andy, and he punched me in the stomach. I got the wind knocked out of me, too. For you! And who was the first person to sign your cast? Me! And remember what I wrote, Pam? I do. "You're awesome. Never forget that."

I can't believe you told people about the note! You have no idea about any of it, and here you go reading a note that friggin' said "TO MATT" on the front, and then you tell people? You know how fucked up that is? You could have really messed up my life, Pam.

I never understood why people talk about other people. It's just not how my mom and dad raised us. And after being with my brother over Thanksgiving break, I learned a lot about a lot. Not that I would share any of it with you because I don't trust you anymore, Pam.

Next time you are thinking of raking someone over the coals, maybe think about that person first. That person has feelings just like you, Pam. If you were so curious about me and my life, why didn't you just ask me, huh? This isn't *Tiger Beat*, Pam.

I'm glad the gossip stopped. My brother and I even played street hockey with Chris and his friends, but I probably shouldn't even be telling you that because I don't know how you will spin it and pass that around. Anyway, what's done is done. I hope you have a good life.

Matt Bloom

Um, hi Matt,

I waited down your street 'til exactly 8:30 P.M. Thanksgiving night. You never showed. And the heat in my Wagoneer broke so I was freezing, but good thing I keep my trunk stocked with a blanket (you know which one as we stargazed on it at Camel Lot), my parka, a scarf, and my old pair of Freaky Freezies. Gloves that change colors in the snow much like people who change WHEN it snows. TGID (Thank God It's December), one month closer to getting the hell outta this tricky town. We live in Opposite World here. Up is down, left is right, and certain Freshmen behave like they're not Freshmen.

Matt, I waited down your street and YOU NEVER SHOWED UP! I then left you message after message on your answering machine. 877-4267. I dialed that number so much I fear I'll never forget it. And trust me, I want to forget it. Why wouldn't I, Matt? You left me in a Thanksgiving Break Lurch!

What's the scoop here, pal? I apologized to you. I made a note-passing mistake. This just in: I AM A HUMAN BEING. I am not this perfect girl everyone thinks I am. I'm just not, ya know? Do you know what I mean?

How was my Thanksgiving? Well, thank you so very, veeery much for askin'. How sweet of you. The sign of a real friend. Is that what we are, Matt? Friends? More than friends? Two people who share something deep? Or just two random people who happened upon each other's lives when one of us was rolling out the plan for her final year in this town, which did not in any way, shape, or form include you!

My Thanksgiving. Well . . . I would love to sit here and say it was incredible and that my aunts and uncles and millions of cousins came in and we all cuddled on the couch and laughed about all our memories, but alas, that is just not my story, Matt.

Yeah, my aunts and uncles came and a handful of cousins, but everyone only comes because they feel like they have to and no one even likes each other. Especially my parents.

Ever since my gramma died the family has completely fallen apart, and all the "True Colors" (one of our songs, Matt, unless it's not. Is it?) have revealed themselves. It's like, don't come for Thanksgiving just because you are honoring a dead woman. "But Gramma Maureen woulda wanted this." On what planet would my gorgeous gramma have wanted her awful family to force turkey down their necks when they'd all be happier at their own houses? Life is so weird, and I feel like a pawn in it sometimes. Like life is just one big chess game, Matt. So . . . if it is a chess game . . . what's your next move?

This is way not my style, but hey . . . I am offering you the ball, Young Man. Ball is in your court.

Write back as swiftly as you can, because depending on what you write it might just alter the course of the last weeks of 1991.

Fondly and Quite Curiously,
Tara Maureen Murphy

Dear Tara,

I hope "True Colors" is always one of our songs, no matter what happens.

I didn't know what to expect when I started here at South High. I don't think I expected anything, really. I had an awesome summer at my overnight camp, and a bunch of my bunkmates were gonna be starting high school too, and we just kind of didn't really talk much about it probably because we were just having a great time at camp. So other than getting a new backpack and some new jeans, I just showed up here.

I guess I had an idea of what it was going to be like because my brother, David, went here, and so I knew about it through him.

Sorry to hear that your Thanksgiving wasn't good. That does suck. Mine was really good. Sorry. Is that okay to tell you? Just being honest.

My brother was home and that was awesome. We hung out a lot and we talked a lot. He told me about everything that's going on at Syracuse, and I told him about everything that's going on here. It was pretty eye-opening. He's a Freshman in college and I'm one in high school (well, you know that, duh), and so we actually have a ton in common right now. He said college is great because you finally get to be on your own and be who you are. I'm definitely not on my own because I live at home, but I do feel like I am who I am. David said he agrees and he thinks I've always been who I am because I always had focus. And he's right, even though I never thought about it that way. I've always known I want to be an actor, and I've always pursued that and worked hard at it even if people made fun of me for it. I just don't really care about what other people think.

I did care about what happened with your note. That made me wicked mad because it's none of anyone's business. Or, it shouldn't have been anyone else's business.

Most of my Thanksgiving break time was spent with my family, my brother, and Joy. I explained the whole thing to her, and she's not mad. She said that the guy who is playing Marius Pontmercy in *Les Misérables* kissed her and she said it was no big deal. I didn't get mad at her. We talked about it. We're both wicked young and we're actors, so it's important to try things out. In a weird way I'm happy Pam Shapiro did what she did because at the end of the day (a *Les Miz* song) it brought me and Joy closer together. She finishes her run as Eponine in *Les Misérables* in February, and I think auditions for the Spring Musical are at the beginning of March, so that's perfect timing for her.

I'm sorry I didn't meet you at the bottom of my street to

go with you to Camel Lot. I do want to know why you call it that and it would be cool to go there with you again sometime. When? I don't know, Tara.

My brother told me to keep my eye on the prize and to stay focused on excelling. He said he wished he had an older brother who could have guided him. If he did, he would have wanted his older brother to tell him not to get involved in any high school bullshit, just pay attention to his own life, his own relationships, and getting great grades. He likes Syracuse, but he thinks if he had been guided more he might have gotten into some other schools.

I got all your messages, and they made me smile. I like being your friend, and I think our relationship as younger brother and older sister is good for us. You have so many years on me and all the wisdom that comes with that. I thought it was so cool in the fall when you shared your opinions about people with me and looked out for me. You were so right, by the way: Heather Gould does kind of suck, and I don't talk to her that much anymore.

You left the ball in my court, so I'm gonna ask you if we can go back to where we were before when it was Tara and Chris, Matt and Joy, and me and you . . . friends.

All my best,

Matt

Oh, P.S. My brother and I played street hockey with Chris and his friends Tzoug and Dube, and it was fun and everything seems normal, and my brother kind of let them know that he's always got my back so no one should really mess with me.

Hey Tara!

What a seriously huge surprise to get a note from you! Like, HUGE SURPRISE! So random, too! Anyway . . . my skin says thanks, ha ha ha.

My Thanksgivin' was average. Nothin' interesting. Thanksgivin' blows anyway 'cuz my dumb family eats turkey all the time, so what's the difference?

Yuh, it's wicked true I'm not goin' to college. Why pay to learn how to get a job when I already have one! I get great discounts at Coconuts and can hook you up like you hooked me up when you worked at TCBY. How good is that white chocolate moose yogurt?!

"Rush, Rush" is such a awesome song, and don't you think that Freshman kid Matt Bloom looks like Keanu kind of? You know the Freshman I'm talkin' about, right? David Bloom who graduated last year's brother. Not that I believed that whole rumor about you guys 'cuz I don't believe nothin' I don't see with my own two eyes, but I know you did *Grease* together 'cuz I saw it. You were wicked good in it, and the girl who played Sandy was unreal. She should be famous. You actors. I wish I could have the guts to act but I don't, and I sing like a farting frog gettin' eaten by another farting frog.

You know me, I'm not into havin' a boyfriend. Hate bein' tied down. But if you know of anyone who's cool maybe I'll think about it. And I gotta be real, I'm not really a Prom girl. Don't get me wrong—I'll go to the after parties, duh, but I don't know about the actual Prom.

Yeah, I don't think I can hang out 'cuz I work so friggin' much. But thanks a ton for the offer. Maybe I'll see ya' at an after-Prom party or something.

See Ya Wouldn't Wanna Be Ya,
Kath

To-est Soup!

You know I have the best instincts ever. Yep, me and my perception-compass. I know you think I'm wrong, but Stef, I am almost positive Kathy and Christopher are hooking up! Oh my god, I am freaking out! I saw her car in his driveway on three different days over Turkey Day break! Unless some-one else drives a Pinto with a license plate that says: LV R TOWN #1, I can guarantee you Kathy is having an affair with MY BOYFRIEND. Do the math, Stef! I saw her grab his ass, and he played it off like she was just being the slut that she is, but I know better. The thought of Christopher touching her makes me literally wanna puke. She said she wishes she could sing, but her voice sounds like "a farting frog eating another farting frog." What girl with any ounce of dignity says "fart"? Or "frog," for that matter? And she had the audacity to say Joy Rebecca Bernstein should be famous! Do you feel as violated as me that once upon a time we were actually friends with such horrific people? As we've grown and evolved these people have just stayed frozen in time. Unreal.

What do I do?

Need You Now More Than Ever,
T-Murphs!

P.S. Not that I care AT ALL, but do you think that annoying Matt Bloom kid looks anything like Keanu Reeves from the "Rush, Rush" video?

To-est Tar,

While Kathy can be gross, and yes, the whole farting-frog thing is appalling, I need you to stay calm!

We don't know for sure that Chris is cheating on you. We just don't know! And unless we have evidence, I do not think it's in your best interest to call him out on it, especially after the November incident. I think you and everyone involved are finally healing from that whole debacle.

So, please take a deep breath, okay? I will keep my ear to the ground, and if Chris is cheating on you we will find out. I really hope he's not. There's no way he is, Tara. He loves you. Everyone knows that.

Jesus, I feel like things are nuts right now with everyone. I mean, here I am about to go on my second date with Diego Conoso, and you think Chris is cheating, and Stacey, who is gonna tell you herself so act surprised please, got dumped by Justin. She is devastated even though they've broken up, like, what . . . 6 times! She said she can't do this anymore even if he begs her to come back. But she will tell you all of this herself. Oh, and to add salt to her wound, she lost her jean jacket. Stacey Simon without her jean jacket just . . . well, it just doesn't even make sense. Wow! We all really need each other more than ever right now, Tara.

Do NOTHING about the Chris sitch. Promise?

Love you, BB MINKEY,

Soup

P.S. Oh, and I can see the Matt Bloom/Keanu resemblance. Actually a lot. Both have long hair and almond eyes.

To-est Mrs. Conoso (tee-hee, tee-hee),

Thank the lord I have you in my world, Stef. Without you I would quite frankly feel I have next to nothin' right now.

You and Diego are gonna go the distance, I can feel it, Stef, and my instincts (which have always proven to be incredibly strong) can feel it, too. Stefanie Conoso has a ring to it, Stef. You always wanted bilingual children!

Oh my GOD about Stacey! It's weird, but I'm not mad at all that I didn't know at the same time you knew. And Stace still hasn't told me, but I am NOT MAD! Crazy, right? I think it's 'cuz we are all friends, and the past is the past, and I trust Stacey and without trust there is nada (that one's for you, Mrs. Conoso)! She better tell me soon, though! And worry not, BB Minkey, I will act surprised, of course. I think if anyone in this town can "act surprised," it's me. (I just thought about how good I would've been as Anne Frank. I've moved on from that, but I still have my moments, Stef, ya know? DYKWIM?)

I double pinky swear not to do anything about the "possible" Christopher and Kathy affair, and I so dearly appreciate that ear of yours bein' kept to the ground. We gotta find out, Stef. I mean, I will find out in a very, veery dignified and mannered way.

As for that Matt Bloom kid looking like Keanu Reeves, all I can say is WHATTTTTT? I simply do NOT see it, and I have perfect vision!

Love you as much as tomatoes love SOUP . . .
Tar

To: Matthew Bloom
c/o Matt who has the number
877-4267
(a number that will, come 1992,
vanish from my memory)

Hello Matt.

What an astonishing note to receive from you. Please don't think by "astonishing" I mean bad or good. I would prefer you not attach any association to the word. Thank you in advance.

If I had asthma I might've needed my inhaler after readin' your note, but lucky for me I've got no health problems. Health is definitely not the department I shop for MY problems in, Matthew. Or is it Matt? Not sure what you're goin' by these midwinter days.

Yeah, Matt, I know "At the End of the Day" is a song from the smash hit *Les Misérables*. I know everything about theater, Kid, so don't you dare attempt to school me on what song is from what show! The nerve of you. I have no idea what the Spring Musical is gonna be, but mark my words, 9th-grader, I will be one of the leads. "Karma (Chameleon)" is on my side ever since that school board canceled *The Diary of Anne Frank*. Talk about gettin' "offered" roles . . . I would've been so good

170

as Anne . . . Broadway would've just OFFERED me a Tony out of respect!

I kindly, generously, and not-needing-to-ly left the ball in your court as sure as my middle name is Maureen (may my Gramma Maureen rest in peace and know always that I carry her name proudly and with it everything—and I MEAN EVERYTHING—SHE STOOD FOR), and I must say I'm stunned how you are playing with it. Again, please don't attach meaning to me bein' stunned. You've simply no idea how I intend my college-level words to land, Mr. Bloom.

A lot of people have been sayin' that you resemble Keanu Reeves from the "Rush, Rush" video. I don't see it. AT ALL. Like, not even a tiny bit!!

I am happy for you that your Thanksgiving was filled with the warmth of family. I think it's wicked clear that you come from a house that's filled with love and support. Maybe too much love and support, Matthew (or Matt), as you have an extraordinarily obscene and unfounded sense of yourself.

So your big brother thinks you're focused, huh? I guess one could argue there's SOME truth to that, Matt(hew), and I should know, as I basically invented tunnel vision. But do you have STAR-FOCUS, like me? Hmmm . . . I'm gonna take a break from this note and go think on it, k?

Hey, I'm back, Matt. I thought. A lot. And you know what, Kiddo . . . you can tell your brother Tara agrees with him full-stop (that's British for PERIOD END OF SENTENCE) about you havin' focus!!

Friends? Us? Matt and Tara . . . friends? I like that. I like the sound of that. I am incredibly happy you ignore Heather Gould now. She's not to be trusted. I guess we can just toss her into the very crowded bucket of "those who can't be trusted"—this town is filled with 'em. But not you, Matt. Nope. I knew from day one I could trust you. Knew it! And through that whole mess last month you proved me right. You could've pointed fingers and made me the bad guy. I mean . . . it was my note that the Giant found. But you didn't. You've handled all of this so gracefully. Beyond your years, Matt. So proud of you. And I'm thrilled you played street hockey with Christopher. I knew that already since he told me (as boyfriends tend to do—they tell girlfriends EVERYTHING), and you know, good for your brother for lettin' everybody know you are not to be messed with. I'll tell you someone else who won't let anyone mess with you, Matt . . . me! Your friend Tara, your "big sis" Tara has got your back always and 4-eva. K?

Now that I'm thinking about it, I guess you kind of do look a tiny bit from certain angles like Keanu from the "Rush, Rush" video. Do you think you do? I'm not a Keanu girl . . . just not into that kinda look, but I bet some people definitely are.

So . . . as my good friend, Matt, could you do me a Good-Friend favor? Would you mind keepin' an eye on Christopher's driveway for me? As you do live across the street I think you definitely have a better view of his driveway than me, who lives across town. Yeah, could ya just let me know if you see a Pinto with the license plate LV R TOWN #1? It's no biggie, I just wanna surprise my gorgeous boyfriend, so if you spot that car call me as fast as you can. Although the heat in my Wagoneer is busted it still drives great, and with my 4-wheel drive I can be across town to your neighborhood in no time! Could ya do me that favor, Matt?

And remember . . . it's for an awesome surprise I have planned for Christopher.

Thanks, Friend.

Always,
Big Sis Tara WHO HAS YOUR BACK

P.S. Although we know I'm not a fan of this Joy Rebecca Bernstein, I humbly surrender the flag. Seems you guys have respect for each other, so . . . just be happy. I only want the best for my friends.

Dear Tara,

I definitely will keep my eye on Chris's driveway. So cool that you're gonna surprise him! You're awesome for so many reasons. I am so happy everything is back to normal for all of us. It's just cool that we can all go away from Christmas/ Hanukkah break feeling good.

Your Lil Bro,
Matt

P.S. Yeah, a lot of people tell me I look like Keanu, but I don't know. Ya know? Do you know what I mean? Haha . . . I'm learnin' so much from you.

Dear Matt,

A lot of people tell you that? Really? Huh. Interesting. Cool.
Thank you for watchin' that driveway for me. I love a good
surprise!

Be Good to You,
Tara

To Matt,

I know we don't know one and other, but you do know my jean jacket because you found it and so kindly brought it to the office. I cannot thank you enough.

My life has been turned upside down and my head has been in the clouds lately. If you knew me you would know I have never once left that jacket anywhere. Where did you find it? I truly have no recollection of where I left it.

Regardless, thank you from the very bottom of my broken heart.

Please let me know how I can repay you for your kindness. Your gesture to this stranger will never be forgotten, and it put a much-needed smile in my heart.

Many thanks,
Stacey Simon
788-7000

JANUARY 1992

Christopher!

So, do you like my hair? I know, crazy, right? Bet you didn't expect to see your blond bombshell girlfriend walk into South High as a brunette. But it's 1992, Christopher. Things change. I certainly have.

I am just so excited for all the "surprises" that are in store for us. What is 1992 gonna bring our way? Who knows . . . guess we'll just have to stay tuned.

I'm so glad we had Christmas together, and oh my god, the Boston Bruins "Have a Great Puckin' Christmas" ornament you got me is so special, I promise, no matter what the future brings, I will put that on every tree I ever have.

We haven't even talked since December 29th. You just disappeared. No calls. No messages. It worked to my advantage 'cuz I just needed to hunker down and finish my outstanding college applications, which I did. Not that any of my backup schools matter 'cuz I'm obviously goin' to NYU, but hey, they are signed, sealed, and delivered. Oh my god, Christopher, in no time flat we will be getting accepted to colleges! It must be so weird for the kids in our grade who aren't even applying to University. How could you not want to make somethin' of yourself? Good thing people like us don't associate with non-college-appliers like them, right?

I love you, Mr. Mister, and I've gotta say . . . I kinda already love 1992!

Your Brunette,

Tara

Tara Maureen!

I saw you earlier, but you were surrounded by a bunch of your friends and I had to get to class so I didn't stop to say hi, but you look AWESOME! Your brown hair looks great!

Happy New Year!

Matt

Matty Matt!

Happy New Year to you too, Fella! Adorable that you think my hair is brown. Such a Frosh thing to say. It's chestnut, Cutie Pie.

Thank you again for calling me when you saw the Pinto in Christopher's driveway. I got to zip over quick as a stick and snap some photographs of him and his friend. I'm waitin' for the film to develop at Medi Mart, but I think it should be ready pretty soon. Then I can surprise the one and only Christopher Caparelli!

So you love my new hair color? Thanks. Everyone is sayin' that. I didn't dye it for attention (god knows I get enough of that), but everyone is stopping me to comment. It grew over the holidays, too, so I guess everyone is just trying to make sense of Tara 1992.

What's the good word by you? How are you and Joy? What did you guys do for New Year's? Elope? J to the k, Matt. Did you? Kidding. But what did you guys do?

It feels good to be back in these hallways, as I know I won't be here much longer. Thank GOD for that! But I had so many realizations over Xmas break. And I made so many New Year's resolutions, Matt. One of 'em was: Enjoy these final months at South High. Just enjoy 'em. So I'm gonna.

I wanted to start things off on a new foot. Well, not literally, Matt. But metaphorically—hence, my new hair color (chestnut!), and if I pass you later you can smell my new perfume! I know, nuts, right? I put my Trésor on the shelf. Didn't want to smell like 1991. Didn't want to be reminded of all the chaos that year brought my way. And we all know I would never wear Anaïs Anaïs again because you bought it for Joy and, well . . . we know that whole old, ancient, unimportant story. I can't believe I remember that even, it seems like so long ago. That happens, though, when the ball drops and the year changes . . . You know? Do you know what I mean?

Really glad you and I are startin' 1992 off with a clean slate, no drama between us, just good friends who HAVE EACH OTHER'S BACKS.

If there's one person besides Stef that I can count on to NOT betray me it's you, Matt.

Always,

Tara 1992

Dear Stacey,

I just had a flashback of our day in Harvard Square. You're right, we did get really lucky it snowed that day. That place is beautiful, but in the snow it's incredible. It was the kind of day you want to put in a snow globe so you can have it forever.

You have to remind me of the songs on your mix. That was the best mix ever! That one song, um . . . number 3, I think . . . something about . . . turning the flowers? Laying down? Remembering? Do you know which one I'm talking about?

I made you a tape of two of my songs. Can't believe I actually played them for someone. But thanks for asking me and for liking them.

So grateful we found each other. I guess we can thank your jean jacket.

Matt

T—

Brown hair, blond hair, long hair, short hair, no hair . . .
doesn't matter. You're the most beautiful girl this town has
ever seen.

Yeah, sorry about not calling those few days. I was just
doing the same as you . . . applications, applications, applications!

Love ya,
C.P.C.

Christopher,

Awwww . . . your few words are the sweetest.

Of course you were buried in college applications, too. Duh. I shoulda known that. My profuse apologies for thinkin' you were, like, I don't know, cheatin' on me. Like you would ever do that!!

The Niña, the PINTO, and the Santa María . . . sorry, another Christopher and his ships just popped into my head. Guess my mind is on history right now!

xoxo,
Tara

Tara,

SohCahToa just popped into my head. Haha.

C.P.C.

SOUP!

Aren't you so proud of me for still not reacting to the "possible" Christopher and Kathy affair? I have to stop putting "possible" in quotes, Stef, I saw the two of them with my own two eyes! That Kathy Connery struttin' around in Christopher's hockey jersey with one of the sides pulled down over her shoulder like she was in friggin' *Flashdance*. I mean, come on, Lady. She might have better skin now, but does that really make up for all the years she didn't? She wore his friggin' skates, Stef. With the blade guards, but still! She kept fallin' all over the place, but I know she loved that because every time she lost her balance, who was there to catch her? MY BOYFRIEND! And Chris had the audacity to do his shy face with her. Like "I know I'm 6 feet and I have a six-pack and I'm an awesome athlete and wicked popular, but I'm just wicked shy, too." Gimme a break, ya' Kit Kat bar. Watching them kiss made me so friggin' sick, Stef, I'm just lucky I didn't crash-land from the grill I was standin' on. Ahhhhhhhhh!! This town!!!

Soon I will have the developed photos to prove it. Why does Medi Mart take forever to develop film?

We need a plan, Stef!! When I pick up the photos, what do I do?

God, seein' you and Diego holdin' hands in the caf made me remember when my own life was pure and simple. When love was the centerpiece of my super full existence. You and Diego make it all look so easy, ya know. A beautiful girl, you, a handsome boy, Diego, in love. Here I am on the verge of the biggest breakup this town has ever seen and my best friend has just entered into the greatest relationship she's ever known. I would say that my impending breakup with Christopher will be bigger news than Stacey and Justin's breakup, don't you think? It better be, not that I care, but it better be.

How is Stacey, by the way? Still super shut down and not lettin' anyone in? I've gotta check in on her. See, even when my life is up in the air I manage to make room for everyone else. One of my resolutions was to stop doing that, but it's a challenge for me, Stef. I care about my friends so much!!

Write back SOONER THAN SOON!

Love you MORE THAN DIEGO LOVES YOU (remember that, k?),

Tar

Dear Matt,

You were so close on song number 3. When I get a chance I will write out the words for you.

But just so you know, that song is titled "Lay Me Down" by the Connells.

You'll have to come over again, and we can listen to a bunch of my records. Also, our grand piano is anxiously awaiting your return. I don't think anyone has ever played it except for you. I used to pass by it and just stare, always admiring how beautiful she was but never connecting to her. Pianos are like works of art. The woodwork. The wires. The keys. So beautiful, but she had this empty beauty until you played her. Now she's alive and has a story to tell.

Thank you for recording your songs for me! That means the world to me. I will honor your songwriting secret always and treasure that you entrusted me to be your first fan.

Our day in Harvard Square is on my top-ten list of best days ever. I love what you wrote . . . it was a day you wish was in a snow globe so you can have it forever. That might be the start of one of your new songs. Think about it.

My jean jacket meant everything to me but that it brought you into my life makes it mean even more.

How are you? How's your heart? Mine is feeling better and better, thanks in huge part to you.

Big hug,
Stacey

To-est Tara,

You don't know that you and Chris are going to break up. You just don't know. Yes, you saw him and Kathy with your own two eyes, but are you sure, absolutely positive, they weren't just hanging out? Maybe Kathy wants to play hockey and so he was helping her with equipment? And if she was on skates and fell into him maybe it's not that they kissed but that they kind of smacked faces. I guess this is my wishful thinking, Tara. Like what if you get the photos back from Medi Mart and Chris and Kath are just talking in them, or watching TV? I am just trying to find the hope here, Tara.

I know your heart so well, and I know it is hurting right now. I know you dyed your hair chestnut because of anxiety, and it looks beautiful, but my hope is that when the photos come back and this gets resolved you will feel like you again. Not saying you have to go back to being blond, but please give yourself the permission to, if you want.

I don't want me and Diego to be a painful sight for you, Tara. We want you to be in our lives, so please find the space in all that's going on to be a part of our world. We both care so much about you!

Stacey is still reeling from her breakup with Justin. I think. I haven't spoken too much to her about it. You know how private she is. She is like a safe-deposit box. But I just keep sending positive vibes her way. I know you are, too.

I will go with you to Medi Mart, okay? We can see these photos together and make some rational decisions from there, okay? And I am proud of you, Tara. You have handled this so well so far. You can go the distance, I just know it.

Love you Muchly and Moreso,
Stef

Stef,

I wasn't sayin' I'm not thrilled for you and Diego 'cuz I am, Stef, I am! Yes, yes, I would love to be a part of your world once mine is not bein' pummeled by a friggin' asteroid, k?

And FYI, I dyed my hair chestnut because I'm an ever-evolving actress, Stef. How can I honestly play brunettes if I've no idea how they feel, how they go about their days? You'll recall I chopped my hair years ago for the role of Connie Wong, and while I did land Anne Frank I would almost be embarrassed tellin' the people at my NYU audition that I wore a wig to garner that role. I don't think the NYUs of the world look kindly on wig-wearin' actors, ya know? Do you know what I mean?

Anyway . . . I am so thankful you are comin' with me to Medi Mart. And not to be rude, but Stacey could at least reply to one of the ten notes I've given her. I get that she's private, but come on. I still think she's awesome, but seriously? Has she even told you who found her jean jacket? I thought she would dissolve without it, so whoever found it is awesome.

Hearts and Stars, my Best Friend,
Tara

Hey Tara—

So sorry I didn't write back sooner. You were right when you told me back in September (of 1991 . . . which does seem like a million years ago, and how do you like my parentheses? Really getting the hang of them. I'm finally figuring out how to use them the right way. Guess who I learned that from?) that life in high school is a whole other ball game. I have so much homework it's nuts, and then everything else in my life . . . it's all so much.

I got a whiff of your new perfume the other day. Really nice. Different. What is it?

No, Joy and I didn't elope over Christmas break. We actually did the opposite. We broke up. We are still really good friends, but her life is so insane with *Les Misérables* closing soon, she just needs to focus, which I understand completely.

And it turned out really good, opened up space for some new things in my life, which have made me really happy.

Anyway, tell Chris I say hi.

Best wishes,
Matt

MATT!!!!!!

OH MY GOD! Stop the PRESSES! Hold the PHONE!
Rewind the VHS! Joy dumped YOU?! If I was someone who
didn't know what to say I would be friggin' speechless right
now, but fortunately for me I have words, lots of 'em, and I
always know what to say! So here goes.

First of all, you and me (us very GOOD FRIENDS) are
so incredibly similar. I've been hidin' my true emotional
state these days because of something so HUGE . . . Oh,
Matt . . . it's somethin' I would love to share with you, but
it would likely best be shared at Camel Lot (only place in
this janky town where things can be shared and not over-
heard), so do consider making time in your busy schedule.
(I shoulda warned you, second part of Freshman year gets
intense, so get used to it—this is a signal of what high school
is really like, okay?)

I know you, Matt. I would say I know you better than anyone at South High. That's for sure. And I know your beating
heart. It's young and naive, yes, but man, is it real. And I know
that you are just sayin' you're cool and happy with Joy dumping
you to save yourself. It's our armor, Matt. Rare people like us

(STARS) build walls to protect the biggest hearts any human beings have ever had. I bet if we talked to some scientists and let them study me and you they would find that yeah, we have the world's biggest hearts. Do you know any scientists? Or maybe your parents do?

My Gramma Maureen used to tell me, "Tara, my Tara, you are special." And you know what, Matt, had my Gramma Maureen lived to meet you she would have said the same of you. You are special, Matt. We are special. And this Joy Rebecca Bernstein (the most conceited Sophomore in the history of time) has some nerve playing you like a fiddle.

Matt, I hate to break this to you, but I bet you are already thinkin' it—Joy is most likely involved in a sordid sexual entanglement with Marius Pontmercy. She's Eponine, Matt! And we know what happens backstage. We've lived it. So wow, Joy gets a regional show and you support her and she goes and cheats on you?! She goes and has an affair with an actor who is not even close to bein' as talented as you! No, I haven't seen the production (like I would pay to see Joy Rebecca Bernstein butcher one of my most treasured theatrical roles, thanks but no thanks), but we know my instincts, and they are stronger than ever these days.

I am not gonna say I told you so, but Matt, I warned you about Joy. She is conniving and potentially evil. Oh my god, THIS TOWN!! Who put this place on the map? Who thought

it was a good idea to invent a town where so many heartbreak-
ers could coexist with people who just wanna love and be loved
in kind? I'm tellin' you, X'ing out days in my Month-At-A-
Glance is gonna take on new meaning now, Matt.

So, you're devastated. We know that. Are you eating? I am,
but skippin' some meals because of my heartbreaking news,
which I will share with you but only at Camel Lot. I think we
could use a good-friend trip there, Matt. We are all we have
left. Well, and Stef, who is my cherry Life Saver.

I am absolutely crushed for you, my Matt. Heartsick. Talk
to me. Let me into your broken heart. I'm not a nurse or a
tailor, but I can stitch it back.

Always and forever,

Your Good Friend. Your Big Sister. Your
once-was-somethin'-else and your possible-once-again-at-
some-point-someone-else,
TARA MAUREEN MURPHY

Dear My Big Sis—

You are the best! Thank you so much for having my back, but I'm seriously fine. I mean it. I love Joy (right now just as a friend, but I do love her). I do not think she is having any kind of sordid thing with the guy playing Marius Pontmercy. I really don't. She has always been really honest with me and I have always been really honest with her. Remember when the whole note thing happened? I know it's a long time ago now, but just remember I told Joy the truth and she told me she and Marius kissed. Once. And she wasn't into it. She really is just focusing on the last few weeks of *Les Misérables*, and I completely get it. Us actors need that concentration. You get that, right? Being an actress and all.

But thank you for having my back even though there's nothing to have my back about. You're the best!

I'm definitely here for you with whatever is going on. Are you okay? I guess you'll tell me at Camel Lot. I will let you know when I have some time to go there with you.

You're awesome,

Matt Bloom (your younger bro)

Sweet Soul-Crushed Matt,

Wow, your walls must be made of cinder block. I don't own a decoder ring, but I don't need one to crack what you're really saying, Matt. Joy has destroyed you. You are feelin' beyond repair. I hate this for you. I hate that she did this to you. Want me to confront her?

When can you go to Camel Lot?? Tell me ASAP!!

Your Protector,
Tara

Tara,

I can go to Camel Lot tomorrow after school. I look forward to hearing what's going on with you, and I hope I can help in some way.

As for me, I swear to God I am happy and fine and great. I promise you I am being beyond honest. Please do not confront Joy. She's amazing and I love her, but again, just as a friend right now. Everything for me is really, really good. The new things that have come into my life are incredible, and I feel truly grateful.

Matt

Matt,

You keep mentionin' "new things" in your life. Can't really imagine what "new thing" would be makin' someone in your position so fine and happy.

Guess you'll tell me at Camel Lot. Pick you up at the bottom of your street at sundown tomorrow.

And don't you worry, time heals all wounds.

Truly,
Tara

Stef,

Thank you more than life for coming to Medi Mart with me last night. Q believe those pictures? Qwe believe this is real? And so it is . . . Christopher is having an affair with Kathy Connery, and now, Stef, now we have developed pictures that prove it.

I did exactly what you told me. Meditated on what to do. And I woke up in the middle of the night with my final decision.

I AM GOING TO RUIN CHRISTOPHER PATRICK CAPARELLI!

I don't give a shit about taking down Kathy Connery—she has no future anyway. But Caparelli . . . that's a whole 'nother story. He's got no idea what I have in store for him!!

Stef, I'm gonna need you to talk to Stacey for me. I know she is still shutting us out because of Justin, but I need you to find a way to communicate to her that I am gonna need her support. Having the most beautiful/popular girl in this town on my side when the shit hits the fan is gonna send a very strong signal to everyone: Chris Caparelli can't just go around cheatin' on Tara Maureen Murphy and get on with his life, eXXXXpecially when Tara has Stef Campbell and Stacey Simon on her side!

Stef, if it wasn't for you plowin' down Stacey Simon on Nantucket I would never be in this power position. I can't thank you enough. You should ride over popular people more often (tee-hee, tee-hee)—thank god I'm gettin' my sense of humor back. (I know you must be like, "There's my Tara.")

This has been such a tryin' time, Stef. But it's almost over. Thank you for bein' you, and tell Stace I thank her in advance for bein' on my side.

I LITERALLY LOVE YOU!

Tara

Um, hey Matt,

What's up, Kid? The funniest thing in the history of New England just happened . . . I just saw you talkin' to Stacey Simon. At first I saw you guys from a distance (you know F Hall . . . long as a summer's day), and I was like, "Maybe Matt Bloom lost his way in this huge school. Maybe he needed an early dismissal slip so he was goin' to Mr. Flaherty's office but he got lost and couldn't find it and so he asked a Senior for directions and the reason Matt Bloom and the Senior were laughin' was because the Senior recalled her days of bein' a Freshman and gettin' directionally confused, too. So they were laughin' because of that common ground." But then as I got closer and things came a bit more into view, I was like, "Did Matt Bloom just hug Stacey Simon? That's not a typical thing for a lost FRESHMAN to do to a SENIOR, let alone a SENIOR such as STACEY SIMON. Hmmm . . ."

You do know that Stacey Simon is a very dear friend of mine, right? She's wicked private and is goin' thru sooo much right now, and well, Matt, you can't just go around huggin' Seniors, hon. I'm wicked protective of my closest friends, and Matt . . . even though she's Stacey Simon she is a person, too. She breathes and feels and has ups and downs just like everyone.

Sooo, what's the scoop here? Were you sad and just needed a hug from the first person you saw? You shoulda come to me, Silly.

Tara

Hey Tara—

Oh, you did? You saw Stacey and me talking? We had a pact
that we wouldn't really talk in school, but we didn't think
anyone could see us, but . . . well, I guess you did.

Okay. Stacey and I have been hanging out. Long story, but
she had lost her jean jacket (not sure if you knew that) and I
happened to be the one who found it and we just got to know
each other through that and stuff.

I know she is a wicked private person. So am I. She and
I definitely have that "common ground." We wanted to keep
our relationship to ourselves. But . . . well . . .

See you at sundown at the bottom of my street!

Matt

Stef,

Did you know Stacey and that annoying Matt Bloom kid have been hanging out? Did you know that he was the one who found her jean jacket? Did you know all of this and keep it from me? Who are you? I am in such a state of shock right now I am actually for the first time in my life speechless.

Not sure why I'm even telling you this, but I am aborting my mission to ruin Christopher. Change of plans.

Later,
Tara

Rick, Allen, Joshua . . . GODDD, what is your name? Rat, Fat . . . oh yeah, Matt.

Are you outta your Freshman mind writin' me that you'll meet me at the bottom of your street? Not in this lifetime, Kid!!

Couple a things: Stop copying how I use my (parentheses), and can you transfer to another school?

Tara Maureen Murphy-Caparelli (SENIOR!!!!!)

P.S. Oh, you're not sure if I was in the know about MY VERY GOOD FRIEND STACEY SIMON losing her jean jacket? I invented bein' in the know, you child!!

Dearest the Most Gorgeous Man in the Western Hemisphere,

Christopher, I love you more than anyone has ever loved anyone. Without you I am just some random brunette. I've been thinkin', Christopher. Remember that claddagh ring I was admirin' at Shoppers World? I know you had said once that you would buy it for me to prove to the town that I'm your girl. I wasn't ready for that then, as I was foolish and immature. It's 1992, C.P.C. I've grown up so much you just wouldn't believe it. I'm ready for that ring now, My Six-Packed Man (you are like Pac Man but Six-Pac Man . . . get Atari on the phone!). I am ready for this town to know that I am YOUR GIRL! So . . . what'd'ya think?

I love you and you make me a better person.

Your Girlfriend . . .
Tara

P.S. I am dying my hair back to blond!!

FEBRUARY 1992

Dear Mi Amor,

I just keep lookin' down at my hand and smilin'. I honestly might have to start wearin' sunglasses at all times, Christopher, 'cuz my claddagh ring is just so shiny!

I can't express in words what this ring makes me feel, but god love-a-duck, I will try. Here goes nothin'.

Christopher, I feel official. I feel like this ring is the first thing in my whole life that gives me a wicked strong identity: I AM YOURS! That feelin' of bein' someone's forever-love is just overwhelming. I can't help but reflect on things, and when I do I just feel so proud of us. We are so unbelievably strong as a Supercouple I believe South High should consider teachin' a class about how to be a powerful couple, one that can weather all storms, and use us as the curriculum example. Maybe we can even come back from college next year and pop in to teach for a day. Yeah right, like I'd ever come back to this school once I graduate. But actually, one just simply never knows.

It just feels so right and so very, veeery relievin' having my ring to look at. It's my lighthouse, Christopher. That great beacon light that can guide me home . . . to you. I gotta tell you, Mr. Mister . . . this month was gonna be so challenging what with two-a-days for cheerleading, but I'm not even sweatin' it now . . . bring on the double practices, get me to Nashville so I can win that national cheerleading title! Now more than ever I have a reason to fight for it. I wanna make my guy proud.

Your Ring-Wearin', Blond-Again Girlfriend,
Tara

Tara Baby,

You blond again make a-me a-very a-happy! And yeah, the ring looks friggin' awesome on you. Glad you like it. That would be funny having a class about us. You're smart. NYU is gonna be lucky to have you.

Lova ya,
C.P.C.

To-est Tara,

I will tell you one last time . . . I knew nothing about Stacey and Matt Bloom! Nothing! And I truly do not understand how their relationship, whatever it may be, has made you so incredibly mad at ME! I don't get it. And I have to tell you I am getting tired of this. We are lifelong friends. Doesn't that count for anything? At what point in a friendship can you just trust the friendship? How many years, decades, does that take?

I've heard your ring is beautiful. Perhaps one day I can see that for myself.

Love,
Stef

Hi Stefanie,

How are you? What's goin' on? How are things with you and Diego? How is your family? Are you all planning your next trip to Nantucket? So many questions, I know, but then questions are, in fact, the key to gettin' answers from someone you just don't see anymore.

Thank you for hearing how beautiful my claddagh ring is! That is so sweet of you to say. I am not one to comment on my own ring, but I agree with everyone that it is quite beautiful. It's 14-karat, so . . .

It feels just wonderful to be, well, basically engaged to Christopher. No, I am not planning my wedding yet, but let's just say I am tearing out some pages from some magazines. Just to have in a file for the when of it all, ya know? Do you know what I mean?

Things are very different once your boyfriend buys you a ring. Things just slow down, and so much that seemed so big and important fades away.

Just when I thought I had a busy life, things got even busier. I am certain you're aware (as the whole town is) that

Nationals are around the corner. Nashville, here I come! I'm definitely gonna buy my closest friends cute Nashville stuff there. Like key chains and magnets. Just little trinkets, forget-me-nots, knickknacks (and paddy-wacks) to bring back for them so I can share my long journey with them. I love gifting super good friends. I'm so like that, though . . . always wantin' my closest to experience things along with me. I've even let some of my good friends try on my ring. I time them 'cuz you never know what kleptos are capable of when given enough leeway. But nonetheless they get to experience what I am feelin'. It's nice to share gifts, rings, and INFORMATION with close friends. Are you into that, Stefanie, or nah, not really?

You mentioned me bein' mad about Stacey Simon and that Freshman kid's "relationship." Oh, dear Stefanie, I haven't even thought about it. Why . . . is it big news around here? Not that I care.

I absolutely hope to meet up with you one of these days and have a catch-up. I used to loathe catch-ups (as you might recall), but now, as a ring-wearin' girlfriend, I've a newfound respect for them, especially 'cuz I'm the only one in this stage of life so I get the responsibility I have to those who aren't quite there yet. And I am playin' with the idea of throwin' a "basically engaged" party for me and

Christopher, and if that comes to light I will beyond consider invitin' you, k?

All my best to you and Diego,
Tara

Tara,

I am worried about you. I have talked to my parents at length about this, and they are worried about you, too. We are here for you, Tara. We have always been a second family to you, and we always will be.

We are worried about you staying with Chris. Look, you know that I wanted, more than anything in the world, for the Kathy and Chris thing to have been wrong. God, Tara, I was praying you were wrong. I was convinced you had it wrong. All wrong. BUT YOU DIDN'T! You were right. Kathy and Chris are having an affair. And as you said, "Now we have the pictures to prove it."

You know I was so blown away by how gracefully you had handled that. You were calm and collected. You meditated on it! That's a big step for you. Not just you, Tara. For anyone. Meditating is not easy, but you did it! You considered things and you were ready to take action.

Look, I am so happy you didn't "ruin" Chris, because come on, we are graduating high school soon, we are too old to "ruin" people, but I understood completely your desire to take him down. I get it, Tara. Who wouldn't? It's beyond not cool that he's cheating on you. If he wants to hook up with other people, fine! Then he should be a man and break up with you. I've never understood the cheating thing. Not on tests, not on people. Just communicate. Why don't people just communicate? Why aren't you communicating with me? Are you shutting me out because of Stacey and Matt?

Look, I know you had a bizarre moment with him. I know you started to have weird feelings about him, but that was for, like, what, a minute? And that ended. Right? So Matt Bloom found Stacey Simon's jean jacket and he returned it to her. And they started to hang out. She is single. He is single. I just don't even understand what the big deal is. Tara, we don't even know what their deal is anyway. Stacey is private, and I respect that. She went through so much having such a public relationship with Justin. Everyone in town, like, fed off of them. Every move they made was looked at and talked about. Don't you get why whatever she has with Matt is something she wants to keep to herself? I do. And she deserves some privacy. You know her now. We both know Stacey is a good person. She's just like us, Tara. Just a Senior girl trying to navigate the last months of high school.

And look, maybe this isn't about Stacey and Matt. Maybe you are shutting me out because you knew I would eventually write this note to you. Maybe you knew I would have a big issue with you staying with Chris. I care too much about you, Tara, to watch you put all your self-respect in the trash. You're wearing a claddagh ring now? Come on, Tara. What are you doing? The more you wear that ring and flaunt your relationship with Chris, the more he gets away with CHEATING ON YOU. Now, do you have to "ruin" him to make your point? Of course not. Do you have to plaster the pictures of Chris and Kathy all over town? No! And I am so happy you didn't do that. But you can communicate with Chris. You can tell him that you know what he's been up to. And you can tell him that you are Tara Maureen Murphy! And the Tara Maureen Murphy I know would dump his ass! I don't want to see you tarnish everything you've worked for. We're so close to the finish line, Tara. Why chuck your reputation out the window now?

I'm here for you. If you want to come over, my mom would love to make dinner for you. We can all sit and talk like the old days.

And as for Nantucket, my parents offered us the cottage as a graduation gift. Think about it.

Love always,

Soup

To Stefanie,

I'm afraid you're barking up the wrong tree. I'm more of a redwood. I think you're lookin' for a weepin' willow. And do thank your parents for me. So kind of them to be "worried" about me. They always seemed like fine people, but you can gossip to them that Tara is doin' just great. You can tell those parents of yours Tara has never been so good, so secure, so sure. And I got a mom who can make me dinner. I got parents, too, Stef, and just like me they have never been so good, so secure, so sure. K?

And as for the graduation-gift offer to go to your Nantucket cottage . . . I have no idea what my plans with Christopher will be after we get our diplomas, so . . .

Let's just do this, k, Stefanie? You worry about you and Diego and your world, and I will worry about me, Christopher, and my world. Sorry if mine is more interesting and exciting, but it's mine, so please respect that.

Regards,
Tara

Tara,

You got it.

    Trust me, I won't give your life a second thought.

Good luck with everything.

Stef

Dear Tara,

First and foremost I want to apologize for not being in touch. I finally listened to all the messages on my answering machine, and there were so many kind and considerate ones from you. I very much appreciate you reaching out and checking in on me. And last night I finally read through all your notes. Those, too, were so generous of spirit and thoughtful.

The reason I finally took the time to listen to my messages and read up on all the notes was because I am really on the other side of things now. I feel happier and more peaceful than I've felt in ages.

I know that while we have known of each other for years and years, we don't really know each other all that well. It was nice to sort of re-meet you through Stef. I know you know this, but Stef is just one of the most incredible people in the world. Certainly one of the best I've ever known. And for me, she is hands down the best girl friend I've ever had.

Not sure if you know this, but girls haven't always seen me for me. They seem to have this preconceived notion of who I am or what I believe, but Stef just didn't. I will be forever grateful that she ran into me on Nantucket. And because of Stef I got the great opportunity to get re-acquainted with you. Another reminder in this life that no story is ever over. A reminder that anything can happen and that everything is possible.

It has been so lovely to get to know you, Tara, and while my breakup with Justin took me out of the loop for a while, I hope that this final stretch of high school can offer us the time to really learn about each other.

You and I share a best friend, and I bet once we spend more time together, we will find out that we have a lot more in common.

Thank you again for being so openhearted with me. For taking time to reach out to me over and over again. That means a great deal to me.

Hope all is well,

Stacey

Stefanie,

I am assuming you told Stacey Simon everything and that is why she wrote me a condescending, manipulative note?! Wow. Just WOW!!

Your Ex-BFF,
Tara

Tara,

Not that I owe you a response, because god knows I don't . . .
but no. I have said nothing to Stacey about you. I have said
nothing to Stacey about you and Chris. I have said nothing to
Stacey about Chris cheating on you. And I knew NOTHING
and KNOW NOTHING about Stacey and Matt Bloom.

Goodbye, Tara.
Stef

To the Kid Who Thinks He Looks Like Keanu,

Did someone send you from some heartless, evil planet to come destroy my life!? Who on earth (my native planet) do you think you are, Matt Bloom??

At every turn you have taken my life off course. Every single turn!!

I asked ya to transfer schools. Is that really so much to ask a life-destroyer?!

I swear to god it's as if your life before South High was spent plotting a way to ruin mine. One can't help but think you are in cahoots with people to just . . . what? Wipe me out? Well, wiped out I am. I am tired. Oh so very tired, Matt, but I will not be stopped. I will win this chess game. Yeah, for a minute there the ball was in your court, Kid, but now . . . now you don't even have a court!

Not sure if you're aware that because of you I have lost my best friend. You aware of that? Huh? Because of you I am staying with a boyfriend that is cheating on me. I have to wear a friggin' claddagh ring from a cheating boyfriend because of you, Matt.

So let's just cut to the center of this Tootsie Pop, k? Enough with your ridiculous "I'm so private . . . Stacey and I are such private people" nonsense. You're at South High, Matt. The place where a giant Freshman girl who works at a candy shop found a note and nearly killed my lifelong-built reputation. Nothing is private in this joke of a town. NOTHING. So stop fronting like you're this super sacred person.

How long have you and Stacey been goin' out? Did you become official boyfriend/girlfriend and then start sleeping together or did you start sleeping together first and then become boyfriend/girlfriend? Are you goin' to Prom together and have you already rented a tux? Knowin' you I bet you've already picked out your cummerbund. Doin' a solid color, Matt, or a more actorly one with paisleys? Huh?

You think I have the time to deal with all this? Well, I don't. I'm packing my bags for Nashville, and I am goin' to clear my head (some of us meditate, Matt), and I am gonna win everything at Nationals. EVERYTHING!!

You'd better answer me, Matt. You owe me that much. I will review your note on the plane, and when I return to this town a winner I will take action.

Write Back or Else,
Tara

Dear Tara,

Woah! Seriously . . . woah! There is so much here to discuss, but let me try to help you make sense of some things.

I was not sent here from another planet to destroy you. I know you're joking about that (at least I'm hoping you are . . . sorry for using your parentheses), but no, I wasn't sent to South High to hurt you in any way.

I'm not transferring schools. So you can stop asking me to do that. Again, hoping you're joking about that, but I've gotta tell you I can't really detect when you're kidding and when you're not. You didn't say j to the k, so . . .

I am so confused about you and Chris. Last thing I knew you asked me to call you when his friend in the Pinto was at his house. I did that. I called you. You thanked me because you wanted to surprise them. I thought that was so nice of you, to surprise him. Then you told me you had stuff to share with me and that you would do that at Camel Lot, but you canceled that plan and have been angry ever since.

Don't think I don't see you giving me the finger in the hallways. I see it. And I also see you mocking the way I blow my hair out of my face.

231

And the whole Keanu thing . . . I'm my own person, Tara, and I like me. I'm not trying to be Keanu. It's not my fault I am Hungarian and Russian, which is why I sort of have Asian eyes. Believe me, I got made fun of for my eyes a lot when I was a kid. People said I was adopted and that I should go back to China. I cried about that a lot. But my mom and dad always told me I was a beautiful boy with beautiful eyes, and my brother always beat the crap out of the kids who made fun of me. One time David had a broken thumb and he had this metal cast kind of thing on it, a splint or something. Some dumb, mean kid was making fun of me, and David grabbed the kid and shoved the metal splint into his neck. The kid never said another word to me.

Anyway. No, I'm not this conceited guy you're trying to make me out to be. I have long hair and sometimes it gets in my face and so I blow it out of my face. You really don't need to mock that. That's mean, and I know deep down you're better than that. And if you're not, let me know, because I don't like mean people. Like one of the buttons on Stacey's jean jacket says . . . "Mean People Suck."

And about Stacey. I didn't plan on my relationship with her. I never even knew her. I had heard about her, but it seems everyone in this school knows about her. But I never thought, "Huh, I should meet Stacey Simon." I was never like, "Hmmm, how can I be calculating and meet Stacey Simon."

The way you're viewing this makes it seem like I stole her jean jacket only to pretend to find it just so I could meet her. Didn't happen that way, Tara. I found something that wasn't mine, and I did what any decent person would do. I brought it to the school office. Lost and found. She lost it. I found it. That's the story and that's the truth.

And Stacey almost never ever talks about other people, but she did say that both you and I were great in *Grease* and that she's happy you guys are friends. That's it. She's said that one thing, and she has never said a bad word about you or anyone. Not even Justin.

No, we're not sleeping together. And no, we are not boyfriend/girlfriend. Stacey and I aren't dating. We're not hooking up. We are friends. Really good friends. And it's a friendship that means a lot to me and to her. And guess what: It is sacred!

Not sure why you and your best friend Stef are in a bad place, but that has nothing to do with me, Tara. Nothing!

I go to school here. I do my best to do well in my classes. I suck at math, but I might be getting a tutor even though I'm begging my parents to just talk to the principal so I can get out of math. I am practicing my new audition songs for the Spring Musical. Auditions are first week of March. I heard a rumor that it's going to be *West Side Story*, which would be unbelievable. Anyway . . . I hope you have a safe flight to

Nashville. I hope you win everything you want to win. I hope I've answered some of your questions. And I hope this drama can stop. It's 1992, Tara.

All my best.

Sincerely,
Matt Bloom

MARCH 1992

To-est Tomato, Minnie Strone . . . Soup!

BB Minkey, this is so unlike you to block my every outreach. But as I continue to reiterate . . . I get it. And man, do I not blame you. I am on my knees literally begging for your forgiveness, Stef.

We are all changing so much as summer-after-Senior-year and first-semester-of college loom over us. I could always count on you taking me back with open arms no matter how crappy I was bein', but you've grown up a ton, and I respect that from the very bottom of my heart. You have blossomed into someone who if I met today for the first time I would envy. Someone I would want so much to be friends with. Someone I would hope liked my clothes, my hair, my thoughts on society and the world at large. You're just so multidimensional and wise and both book- and street-smart. Basically, Stef—you friggin' get it. Whatever the IT everyone always talks about is . . . you get IT and have IT. All of IT.

I just can't bear to go another day having won Nationals and MVP without being able to share it with you. I mean this, those titles and the trophies and the new school banner, mean less than nothing to me because I can't even share it (IT) with you. What's a mansion, they always say, if you can't share it with those you love most? A yacht is just some floating metal if it's not filled with people you love. And titles are meaningless if your best friend isn't in your world.

Pleading with you, Stef. Let me be a part of your world. Mine is nothing without you in it. That I can say for certain.

Ya know, I was so delusional coming into 1992 thinkin' I had "evolved so much" and "figured it all out." I am humbly admitting I don't know much, but I know I love you. (Oh my god, I just remembered how much we sang that song, Steffed Animal. You were the most glorious Linda Ronstadt and I, an amazin' Aaron Neville.)

While I can't do anything until *West Side Story* auditions are over, I am going to listen to my best friend (you might know her . . . her name is Stef Campbell . . . she is, oh, I don't know . . . the best girl ever. Heard of her?) and end things with Christopher. Let me say that again. I AM GONNA END THINGS WITH CHRISTOPHER!

I guess I forgot me along the way. I forgot who I am. What I'm made of. You tried so hard to remind me, but I was basically deaf. You could have done sign language and I wouldn't have gotten it, Stef. I guess that means I wasn't deaf. I was dumb. Ignorant. Arrogant. All of it (IT).

I've changed, though. I have. Going to Nashville, being immersed in Southern culture, changed me. I got to sit and meditate (thanks to you, my guru) and get clear. And clear I am, Stef. Clear as Ms. Bugg's chalkboard after I got picked to squeegie it.

And I miss your mom and her cooking. Why couldn't she have rubbed off on my mom? Things I will probably not understand until I'm in college. There are so many things I bet I just won't have the ability to get until I'm outta this town. All that is to say, Stef, I would LOVE to come over and have your mom's dinner. I would love to talk and do our figure-life-out old-school conversation. And I am not assuming the Nantucket cottage offer still stands, but I can't think of a better way to bid South High an official farewell. In a cottage on an island with my best friend.

I will keep writin' you until you can find it in your heart to forgive me this one last time. Hey, I imagine siblings fight and make up a ton, right? And we are sisters, Stef. So I do hope that counts for a lot.

Diego is so lucky to have you. And while he was very, veeery good-lookin' before, havin' you by his side has made him flat-out gorgeous. I say that simply as a testament to you. You make people shine. I ask to be one of the lucky ones who gets the benefit of your Halley's Comet.

Hearts and Stars and Galaxies . . .
Tara

Dear Matt,

I guess there is no better time to thank you than now, what with the cast list bein' posted on the board and all. Seems Matt and Tara and Joy were destined to share the stage as equals. I think Joy will be a wonderful Anita to my Maria. And you as Tony . . . well, watch out, world!

I can't believe I had the audacity to tell you many moons ago that you wouldn't get Danny Zuko. I only said that, Matt, because never in the history of South High has a Freshman gotten a lead out of the gate. And then you followed that brilliant T-Bird turn with a plush role in *The Diary of Anne Frank*—a show we will likely grieve the cancellation of for a thousand lifetimes. And here you are now in the spring of your rookie year at South High landing the greatest (or at least one of the greatest) roles for a guy in the theater: Tony.

Sure, there have been many a production of *West Side Story*, but Matt, come on, me as Maria and you as Tony!! I just can't fathom any version of this iconic show being as good as what we will deliver come show night! I guess today begins our next long journey together, Matt. This time as co-stars. If you recall, you and I wished for this. We wished to be Danny and Sandy, but alas, the gods chose to make us wait, make us grow, make us learn before putting us together as one of the world's most anthemic fictional Supercouples: Maria and Tony. I simply have no words. Sandy had always been a dream role of mine, and Eponine! Oh, how I scribbled in my diaries that I would be her. But the secret I've been sitting on for the better part of my life is that above all else I wanted to play Maria. You can even ask my diaries. J to the k . . . those are under lock and key and hidden better than Anne hid hers.

I am thanking you because you were so thoughtful when responding to my anxiety-filled questions pre-Nashville. Your calm and soothing answers helped me more than you know, Matt. I got to Nashville a changed girl. I got to breathe for the first time in a long time. I think Nashville has better air than our town (add that to the list of things that are better out there beyond our Mass Pike exit).

And because of you and your classic Matt Bloom pure heart, my squad won Nationals and I was named MVP. Most Valuable Player. Little old me . . . MVP. Who'da thunk it? Gettin' that recognition from the National Cheerleading Association has given me tremendous pause, Matt. I know now that I have an important position here at South High. I'm a leader, and lead is what I intend to do these last months here. I guess getting the LEAD in *West Side Story* is the universe just saying, "Lead, Tara, lead. And don't get off track!" Universe . . . I won't.

You know, it's funny how junk works, Matt. Even in my frustration and confusion I told you that Christopher was cheating on me. You think I would tell just anyone that? No. I told you because I, as I have since day one, trust you. And even when, in my past, I would get wicked mad and fly off the handle . . . even then I knew I could trust you. I will be breaking up with Christopher very soon. I just wanna do it gracefully. We did have something major, he and I. We were a nonfictional Supercouple. But not everything is what it seems. I can say that with certainty now.

I'm heart-warmed that you've found a sacred friend in my dear friend Stacey Simon. That girl is solid, and for me to say that is a humungous deal.

Hey, if I could put my arms around all of us, everyone at South High, and just tell everyone it's all gonna be okay, believe you me, I would. But I have human arms, and they just don't stretch all that much.

I hope me, you, and Joy can work hard and make *West Side Story* the greatest thing to ever hit a stage. As Maria I pledge to keep the vibes great among cast and crew. I'm even bakin' my famous gooey double-chocolate-chip cookies as a welcome treat for everyone.

Someday, Matt. Somewhere, Matt. We absolutely will find a new way of living . . . and you know what else, Matt? We (and I know this as sure as I know I will get into NYU) will find a way of forgiving . . .

Always,
Tara (Maria)

Hi Christopher—

I was hoping we could calendar some face-to-face time. There's something I've got to tell you, and I would like to do it in person.

When are you available?

Thanks,
Tara

Tara—

Wow, we must be psychic. There is something I want to tell you, too.

Will call you tonight to make a plan.

Peace,
Chris

Chris—

Okay, yeah, phone me tonight and we will make a plan.

What do you have to tell me?

Well, I guess we'll make our plan and then I'll find out.

Best,

Tara

Blooming Flower,

I am so happy for you that you got the role you wanted. And what an honor that you practiced for it at my house on our piano. I will be at your opening night, front and center.

I took your advice and gave Justin the chance to share his heart with me, and I am glad I did. He is a beautiful soul, but he has so much to work on for himself. He has so many wounds and I know we all do, but he's never taken the time to really deal with his. And I discovered that I've never really taken the time to deal with mine. That's why this moment in life is so good for me. I've never really been single, so I've never had the chance to see the world through my own lens. And I love what I am able to experience now. Close friendships. Art. I mean, I am drawing again! I haven't drawn for years, and I bought two new sketchbooks and it's pouring out of me. Being your friend has brought art and thought back into my life, and I am forever grateful.

So I left it with Justin that I will always love him. I will always be here for him. And I will always leave the door open for the possibility of getting back together, just like you did with Joy. But for now, right now, I am just falling in love with me and that feels great.

Okay, friend . . . let's hit some art galleries in the city when you can. I know how busy you're about to be, so no pressure ever.

Big Hug, You Blooming Flower of a Human Being,
Stacey

To-est Stef!!! URGENT!!

In no way, shape, or form do I want to rush you through your process of accepting my profuse and now multiple apologies. You take your time, and I mean that. I am right here waiting for you.

I am wondering if you could break your silent treatment to be my best friend for, like, one second.

So, I told Christopher we needed to make a face-to-face plan so I could tell him something. Obviously, you know that something is me breaking up with him. But I am of course going to do that in an adult, SENIOR YEAR way, which is in person. And so when I told him I had to tell him something, he told me that he also had somethin' to tell me.

Then we talked last night to make our in-person plan. He didn't mention what he wanted to talk to me about and I didn't either. But so we are meeting up this weekend. Are you thinkin' what I'm thinkin'? That Christopher is going to fess up to his affair with Kathy and beg me to forgive him? Obviously that's what it's gonna be.

Please, Stef. I need your guru/sister help. Please help me, then you can be mad at me again even though I would be so happy if you weren't, but I understand if you still need more time to be mad. HELP!!

Tara

Tara—

I do still need more time to think about how you and I can go forward in a clean, loving way. But I care about you too much to not lend you my support here.

Yes, I do think you are right that Chris is going to admit to his cheating and plead with you to stay with him. That is the only thing that makes sense. So here is what I will tell you, Tara. Stay strong. You are currently moving forward in many areas of your life, and even though I am still so upset with how you've treated me, I can see that you are growing up. So let this moment with Chris be your greatest science lab yet. Stand strong, be brave, and stick to your guns.

Good luck,
Stef

Stef!

I love you so much! I will stand strong! Oh, you'd better believe it! Thank you for loving me through thick and thin and for taking time out of your silent treatment to help your childhood best friend.

Lives, Loves, Laughs,
T-Murphs, Tmurphette, Tara Maureen!!

Dear Stacey,

Hi sweetheart! I just adored your note back to me, and Stace, don't even apologize for a split second about how long it took you. If anyone in this town knows about boyfriend stuff, breakups, and healing, it's this girl.

As you are a dear friend of mine (and by the way, I LOVE THAT YOU AND I SHARE A BEST FRIEND. AND I KNOW YOU ARE NOT ONE TO TALK ABOUT OTHERS TO OTHERS, BUT WHEN YOU TALK TO OUR MUTUAL BEST FRIEND STEF, PLEASE DO TELL HER HOW MUCH I LOVE HER AND HOW MUCH I LOVE THAT YOU AND I GET TO BOTH HAVE HER AS OUR BEST FRIEND), I wanted to very privately share with you what is going to take place this weekend.

Stacey, I am going to break up with Christopher. I know, huge turn of events, but this is quite necessary. And yes, of course Stef already knows about this, so you don't have to share this with her even though you wouldn't because people like you don't talk about others to others, which I find exceptionally commendable and a real sign of great character.

I just wanted to tell you in advance of the event, because while I feel stronger than ever and more secure than ever, I am a girl with a huge heart, and I might be wicked sad when we break up, and I might shut down just like you did when you and Justin broke up.

I ask you this, Stace. Please do not think I am ignoring you, your calls, or your notes. You and I are so similar, and if I don't respond right away it's not about YOU at all . . . it's just me processin'.

Here goes nothin'.

Tara!

Dear Tara—

It's just not in my comfort zone to tell Stef anything you say to me, even though what you said was so lovely. I just do not pass information and I never have. It's just not me.

But I am really excited for you, Tara. I know that sounds strange, but being on the other side of my breakup I can tell you that it's a whole new world. Being single can be the greatest gift you give yourself. My only suggestion is to remember you shared something special with your boyfriend, so to best honor that I think it is good to lovingly end things and leave space for the friendship that got you there in the first place to be able to come around again.

Be good,
Stacey Simon

Stace!

You are so beyond special. I hope there's room in your single world for me, because I will be joining you.

Hearing that guidance from you means everything. And to hear how amazing your life is now that you are single is so friggin' inspiring.

I pledge to lovingly break up with Christopher and to graciously leave room for a friendship with him.

You rule!

Love you!
Tara "Soon to Be Single and Lovin' It" Murphy

Oh, my Matt . . .

Stef won't return my calls. Stacey takes a thousand years to respond, so I am praying you will find the time in your busy and happy life to get back to me.

How was your weekend? Hopefully filled with love and laughter. I bet you got to spend time with your adoring family, and knowing you, I'm sure you rehearsed your songs for *West Side*. Professional actors like you take advantage of the weekends. Maybe you even talked to your big brother. How lucky you are to have such a close relationship with him. And him bein' at college and still looking out for you is huge and so rare.

Um, me? Thanks for askin'. I, um . . . I had a pretty cool weekend. Yeah, it was okay. Busy of course, but definitely, by all definitions, a weekend.

I know you have so much of your own stuff goin' on and that you have your priorities, like doing well in school and focusing on acting and being in a sacred friendship with Stacey Simon, but if you can dig through your heart and find one tiny, little-little section for me, I would be indebted.

I met up with Christopher so I could break up with him. And I was so calm and loving and therefore I was takin' my time in tellin' him. It's not like I was talking slow, but I was being mindful. Even though he cheated on me I had made my choice to leave him, and I wanted to do that with kindness and integrity. It's just not in my comfort zone to be any other way.

So as I am trying to get to my point and say, "Christopher, I am breaking up with you," he just interrupted me and said, "I'm not sure what you are trying to tell me here, Tara, but it might not be important after I tell you that I am dumping you."

He didn't even say, "breaking up with you," he said, "dumping you."

I was so shocked, Matt, I couldn't even speak. Literally. It was just like that day after the reservoir with Timmy Garabino all over again. And as I sat there in silence he said, "So . . . we good?" And then he said, "Can I have my ring back?"

I was, like, comatose, Matt. I didn't speak. I didn't move. And he just ever so gently slid the claddagh ring off my finger and said, "See ya at school?" Um, where else would he see me, Matt . . . at Disney World? In Paris? In Allentown, Pennsylvania? (My one uncle lives there, so I thought of it.)

I need a friend right now, Matt. And I have a huge favor. It's a favor that actually benefits everyone involved. I have an envelope (it's sealed) of photographs. I do not want them in my house for I fear I will be too tempted to do something harsh with them. You needn't know what the photos are—the less you know about those, the better. But would you just keep the envelope at your house, in your room . . . somewhere no one can find them? If you have them, I won't, and therefore I will be able to move through this without revenge. Could you do this for me, Matt?

Your Devastated Maria . . .
Tara

APRIL 1992

Bloom—

I hope it's okay with you that I joined stage crew for *West Side Story*. I'm not trying to stalk you, I swear—I just wanted to start building up extracurricular credits even though I'm not gonna be doing college applications for three more years but it's not like Fanny Farmer could be considered extracurricular 'cuz it's just a candy shop and it's just my job.

You're so good as Tony! Seeing you and Joy rehearse is so awesome. You guys are seriously the most talented people ever. And I know it's none of my business, but seeing you guys up there together and, like, talking in between scenes makes me wicked happy. I hope you guys get back together because you deserve to and you just belong together. Me and so many other people on stage crew think that, and we think Joy could've played Maria better than Tara, but Anita is such a good Joy part 'cuz it's explosive and just cooler all around. I got chosen to be the crew key keeper! I'm wicked excited 'cuz I love key chains and have a collection of them and also being in charge of the keys to the theater and music room and copy room is just so cool!

263

I wicked hope you will be my friend again one day. I know I messed up big time, but I'd never do anything to hurt you again. I would only wanna help you, not like you need it.

But if ya ever need anything, you know where to find me.

By the way, I will say Tara is a good baker. Her gooey double-chocolate-chip cookies were wicked good. If we had those at Fanny Farmer I bet they'd sell out.

I'm still into New Kids but not as much. Things change. I'll always love Joey McIntyre, but I'm not, like, as obsessed as I used to be.

Keep doin' an awesome job as Tony.

Pammy

Hey Pammy—

Things do change, and so much has changed since last fall. I noticed you were on stage crew. Good for you. That's awesome. Yeah, if you stick with it I bet it will be a really good credit for colleges. And being crew key keeper is a big deal! Congratulations on that.

I'm really happy with how *West Side* is going for many reasons. And you guys on stage crew definitely have a bird's-eye view of what goes on onstage. Joy and I are rediscovering each other in many ways. We needed our break so she could focus on *Les Misérables* and so I could focus on my life. But . . . well . . . let's just say I think when two people are destined for each other nothing can get in the way of that. Sort of the theme of *West Side Story*. Seems everything happens when it is supposed to and for the right reasons.

Can't imagine any favor I would need from you, but you never know. So, thanks.

Take care, and here's a stage crew tip: Be careful around the flats after you paint them. The weight of the wet paint sometimes makes them fall.

Matt Bloom

Dear Matt,

Thanks again for taking the envelope. You are a world-class GOOD FRIEND. You have no idea how good NOT having that in my house is for me and the town itself.

Getting to be Maria is such a savior for me, Matt. And I just totally relate to her. She is in love with someone she shouldn't technically be in love with. But the heart wants what the heart wants. And what Maria wants is dangerous, and she knows her friends look down on it, and she knows that the entire town would freak out if she were to go the distance with Tony. But guess what, Matt? Maria is a strong woman, and she doesn't care what anyone thinks. Tony is the only one in the world that makes her feel alive, and by hook or by crook she is gonna let herself fall for him. I think Maria is as surprised by this revelation as anyone. She was just livin' her life, layin' out her plans. She could never have expected this guy from the other side of the tracks just poppin' into her world and rearrangin' her entire blueprint.

I noticed that giant Freshman note-thief Pam girl on stage crew. As the main lead in *West Side* I have a lot of power (although I don't think of it as power as much as I consider it leadership), but you give me the word and I will have her escorted out of the theater. Is she bothering you? Is her presence in our sacred space an everyday reminder of darker times? You tell me, Matt. Whatever you need me to do, please do trust I will do it and how.

I will say I am pleasantly surprised by Joy's talent. She is pretty darn good. I can't say if she has a future in the performing arts, but she's not half-bad. Are you guys gettin' along okay? I see you crackin' jokes and havin' conversation, but I know you so friggin' well and I know that you are just kind (especially to third leads). I am pretty sure her name won't be above the title on our playbills, but I will check on that just to be sure. And if you absolutely don't want her name above-title like our names, gimme the signal and I will take care of that. She did dump you, and although you were evolved about it, a dump is a dump is a dump no matter how you slice it.

Tickets for Prom go on sale soon. Did you see the banner in the hallway for it? The theme is "Hold On to the Nights." Not sure if you recall, but that's one of the songs I had put on the Camel Lot mix I made you.

I wonder who I'll go with now that I'm single? Kurt Cutter is wicked hot, don't you think? Hmmm . . . who will I go to Senior Prom with? Would you ever in a million, billion years go to a Senior Prom as a Freshman? Not that you're a typical Freshman, but still. Would you? Lemme know just as a question of curiosity. You know me, Matt, I love learnin' new things about you. Who knows, though . . . maybe me and Stacey will just be dates as we're both single and happier than ever! So much success in Nashville, the lead in the most anticipated musical South High has ever done, Prom around the corner, and any minute now I will be receivin' my acceptance letter from New York University (that is long for NYU, Matt. Home to one of the premier acting schools in the country, not to mention the University itself is a stone's throw from the most important place in the world . . . Broadway!) Life as we know it just keeps gettin' better and better, Matt!

Te adoro, Anton . . .
Tara

To-est Tara,

I don't know why, but I needed to share my news with you before I share it with anyone else. Tara . . . I got into Northwestern!!

My parents have never been so happy, and I have to tell you, neither have I!! I know I kind of made the possibility of getting into Northwestern seem like something I didn't care too much about, but now that I've gotten in I can be honest with myself and say I was just shielding myself from the chance I didn't make the cut. I was so worried that my parents would be crushed. But I guess I will never know if my fears were right because, oh my god . . . I got in!!!

Okay, I do know why I had to share this first with you. You are my best friend. And it's only with true best friends that you have this need to tell them great things first. You know, before the parents tell their friends and those friends tell their kids and then before you know it everyone knows. You know first. Just know that.

I can't even believe I will be living in Chicago in what? Five months. Chicago!!! I know you're going to say, "It's freezing there," but I am going on a shopping spree to buy everything

I will need to survive the Windy City. My parents say the first thing we are doing when they move me into my dorm room is unpack, make it pretty, but the first real thing is to go directly to their favorite deep-dish pizza place! I am not going to ask that dreaded question "Have you heard yet about NYU?" But Tara . . . have you? Sorry, that's annoying. I am just excited to know where you will be so we can just know!!

I have to say that when I opened my acceptance letter I started to bawl. Not because I got in but because you weren't sitting with me. We weren't holding hands. We were supposed to be holding hands for every college envelope. So, if you haven't gotten yours yet, will you let me be there, holding your hand?

I have had enough time to process everything between us, Tar. I don't want to be mad at you anymore. I just don't. But I also don't want to start this next huge chapter of our lives going in and out of craziness. Not that we can't argue or even fight . . . that happens. But we can't flat out mistreat each other. You can't flat out throw me away, throw our history and our trust away when you're feeling down. Does that make sense? I love you and our friendship too much for that. And I believe strongly that you do, too.

We have five months left. Not even, as I am going to spend the summer on Nantucket. And yes, the invite still stands. Can we please go to the cottage after graduation?

Diego and I discussed this, and we want to invite you to be our Prom date. I know you're thinking, "Third wheel. No thanks." But it's not like that. It's our Senior Prom. It's "Hold On to the Nights." Let's just go and have the best time ever and hold on to the night. Together. Let me know, okay? And we also have to book a limo from Kurt Cutter's dad. I heard they are already getting rented.

Love you, T-Murphs . . .
Soup

To-est my BB MINKEY!!!

Chicago is about to become the LUCKIEST CITY IN AMERICA!!! I knew you would get into Northwestern and you know I knew that!! I am so proud of you, Steffed Animal!

I am crying right now I am so happy you are letting me back in. I triple pinky swear (what am I, a three-pinkied person? Tee-hee, tee-hee) that I hear you loud and clear. I get it (IT). I really do!

Okay, Miss Northwestern . . . expect a call from me the second I open my mailbox and see my acceptance envelope from NYU, which should be any day now!! You are definitely holdin' my hand, and that is that. (Q believe you're gonna be in Chicago and I'm gonna be in New York City? I knew our hard work and daydreamin' would get us to major cities and far, far away from this provincial town!! I wonder if there's a train that goes right from your dorm to my dorm, tee-hee, tee-hee!! Do you think there is one?)

So sweet of you and Diego to ask me to Prom. You cuties. Let's definitely book a limo (doesn't have to be a stretch 'cuz god knows we don't need extraneous people), but yes, let's book one. Give me a beat to decide about taggin' along with you and Diego, k?

Love you!
Tar

P.S. A million percent YES to post-graduation cottage! I can't wait to see this Nantucket you and Stacey speak so highly of!

Tara,

I am totally fine with having Pammy Shapiro on stage crew. She needs the experience, and I am so far past that time in my life, your life, our life. So, yes, she's fine. Thanks, though, I appreciate you lookin' out for my best interests. It feels really good being back to normal with you. And I love every day we get to rehearse opposite each other.

I'm so relieved you and Joy are getting along. I have been noticing that, and it makes me so happy. Especially because you are a good friend of mine, and Joy is, well . . . let's just say she is very special to me, and I'm glad you guys are getting to know each other.

You know, it's funny about Senior Prom. I thought I would never even consider going to another grade's Prom, but never say never, right? You taught me that. Stacey asked me to be her date. She wants to go with a close friend and just have a great, fun time. It's crazy, but when you were mad at me you sort of guessed this would happen. But under totally different circumstances because Stacey and I are just great friends and nothing more. She said we will be going in a limo with Stef and Diego and you and . . . Kurt Cutter? That would be awesome. I've heard he's a really good guy, and even though Chris is my across-the-street neighbor I think it's time for you to be with a good guy. Ya know? Do you know what I mean?

Te adoro, Maria . . .
Matt

    P.S. My fingers are crossed for you about NYU. Please let me know how that goes?? Of course I know that New York University is long for NYU. That was wicked funny of you, though. It's my number one college choice too (even though it's sooo far down the line. But can you imagine if you were a Senior there when I was a Freshman?)

My Talented Tara,

I am still stunned. I went to bed hoping I would wake up and realize you not getting into NYU was a terrible nightmare. I've never wished for a nightmare to be true more than I did for you, for this.

You had no reaction to the rejection letter, which I thought was such an incredible sign of who you are and how much you've grown! You are so inspiring. Are you sure it's okay that I left when I did? I know you said it was but just double-checking on that.

You have so many more letters to get, and I know you know this, but I have to say again that I have so much faith that so many of them will be ACCEPTANCE LETTERS, TARA!!

NYU's loss, Tara! Not yours!

I love you so much,
Stef

Stef,

I had no reaction because I just sort of went into deep meditation about it. I'm not viewin' the letter from NYU as a rejection letter as much as I am a "You're too good for our school" letter, sooo . . .

Anyway . . . so many more letters to come! And no matter where I end up I for sure hope there's a train from my dorm to yours!

Yeah . . . I'm good, Stef. Wicked chill and calm and not even fazed and stuff.

xoxo,
Tara

Dear Tara,

Any word on your NYU acceptance? Been thinking about that so much! So eager for you!!

Your good friend,
Matt

Hey Matt,

Thank you so much for your wicked eager note!! I know this is gonna probably bum you out tremendously (because of your cutesy vision of us bein' at University together and somehow duplicatin' this whisper-in-time-of-a-year), but alas, I've made the very, veeery deeply thought-thru and composed decision NOT to attend New York University.

So sorry that your vision won't come to light, Matt. While I feel bad about that, I couldn't just go around makin' plans for my future 'cuz of Matt Bloom's hopes and desires. You get that, I know you do.

I'm quite thrilled I finally made my choice as I was ponderin' and ponderin' and you know how I feel about CHOICES, Matt. I make 'em and then I move on! So guess what, M. Bloom? Movin' on.

So OH MY GOODNESS, YOU'RE COMING TO MY PROM!! Between CHOOSING to pass on NYU and news of you goin' with Stacey Simon to MY Prom . . . well, you can imagine how elated I am!!! I'm so elated, Matt, I bet I could fill a banquet hall with balloons that I breathed the helium into from my very own elated lungs!

Well, I for one am just overJOYed, Matt!! Oh my GOD, and that we are all goin' in a limo together?!!! What could possibly make for a more celebratory end of my high school experience? I'ven't a clue!

ALL MY BEST,

Tara

P.S. Who am I goin' to Prom with? You and the rest of the town will just have to wait and see. K?

MAY 1992

To-est my Soup!!!!!

I literally cannot stop thinking about yesterday! Talk about the most unreal and surreal day of my life! I will never ever forget holding your hand (the hand of my best friend) while I ripped open not one, not two, but THREE acceptance letters!!! Oh my god!!! I guess here comes the hard part. Where to go to University?? I know, there are way worse problems to have! I am so beyond glad I didn't "get into" NYU!! First of all, it's not nearly as good a school as people try to make it out to be, and I'll be moving to New York anyway for my career, which is way better than goin' there to attend some average college! I know you agree.

And I swear to god if we hadn't gone for Chinese after (and if we hadn't been through these crazy Senior year ups and downs), we would never have run into Kev Brandolini. My god, does that guy get hotter and hotter. No wonder everyone just calls him Brando. When we first saw him you pinched me 'cuz my jaw was literally in my hot and sour soup, Soup. Thanks for the pinch, by the way . . . wouldn't be the greatest time for a third-degree burn on my FACE!

Stefanie Campbell, I will never forget the friggin' look on your face when I asked Brando if he wanted to go to Prom with me. You almost blacked out! I was totally just kidding with him, but then he said yes, and I was like, "I'm sorry, what?" And you were like, "Wait, really?" Good thing we booked the mid-size limo, Stef, 'cuz Brando is so muscular and tall! Not that Diego isn't, but . . .

Ya know, my fortune cookie was right: "Don't look back or you might fall in the pothole in front of you." And look back on what, even? Christopher cheatin' on me with Kathy Connery? Him breaking up with me and taking back a chintzy claddagh ring? I don't think so. If I were to look back it would only be to thank the past for getting me to the greatest time in my life.

Three colleges accepted me! I'm Maria, for christsakes! And now I am going to Senior Prom with Kev Branolini, who just happens to be, oh, I don't know, the hottest guy this town has ever seen (except for Diego, duh!)!

We have the best limo ever! You and Diego, our dear friend Stacey and the sweet-as-can-be Matt Bloom, and me and Brando! I heard Chris is just goin' stag with Tzoug and Dube. I don't even know if they're goin' in a limo. But, not my business.

I can feel the end of high school, Stef. We are so close! And it's just gonna be smooth sailin' now. We have nothing to worry about except for having a great time. Oh my god, am I grateful you told me not to paper the town with those incriminating photos of Chris and Kathy. I could've destroyed a lot of lives in the wake of that, and for what? Nope. I stayed classy and above it because of you, BB MINKEY. And now "Karma (Chameleon)" is on my side!

Love you, Miss Northwestern,
Tara "Which College Will I Choose" Murphy

Matty Matt!

Hey there, ole buddy, ole pal! I don't want you to be the last
to hear it, as I'm sure this news will be swirlin' around South
High soon enough . . . but not only did I get into my top three
colleges (I know, has that ever happened to anyone? And
thank god I CHOSE to decline NYU . . . they don't even have
a proper campus, Matt . . . sure, people say, "The city is its
campus," but come on . . . there's NO QUAD), but I am also
goin' to Prom with KEV BRANDOLINI. I know I told you
of him decades ago, but to refresh your memory he is older
than me (I know, right?), and he's the most athletic guy ever,
and he just happens to be drop-dead gorgeous. Brando and I
are so thrilled to be sharin' a limo with you and the lovely and
beautiful Stacey Simon (as well as with Stef and Diego—a
dynamic couple in their own right).

Will you do me one last favor? I swear it is my last one ever.
Could you either burn or shred the envelope I gave you? I just
want it gone forever.

Thanks, Tony Tony Tony, and MWAH . . .
Tara

Dear Tara,

It's May, so my dad isn't making fires in the fireplace right now. I guess I could figure out a way to shred the envelope, sure. But why? What the hell is in this envelope?

Awesome about your Prom date. I think I remember you saying something about Kev Brandolini. He's not the jerk that unlocked and opened the car door . . . no, wait, that was Tommy or Timmy something, right? Maybe Kev was the guy with all the Christmas trees? I don't know, but either way it's gonna be such a fun night.

Matt

Dear Matt,

It's gonna be the best night ever! Prepare to "Hold On to the Night(s)." And yes, Matt. Kev Brandolini is the one with all those Christmas trees (and horse stables, etc., etc.), and I've no doubt he will be wicked nice to you and give you the time of day! He's definitely not your typical beyond-gorgeous tall-and-ripped guy who thinks so highly of himself that he doesn't acknowledge other guys just 'cuz they're shorter and not as built. You think I would go to Prom with an arrogant guy like that? NEH-VER!!

Oh god, the envelope, Matt! Okay, so remember when I was being wicked immature a while back? I know, seems like forever ago, and it kind of was. I don't remember much that occurred pre-getting-into-three-colleges. Anyway, when life was chaotic I asked you to call me when a Pinto arrived in Chris Caparelli's driveway. Remember? And you were so sweet to call me and tell me. I kinda fibbed (my Gramma Maureen's favorite word) to you, Matt. I wasn't driving over to "surprise" Chris and his "friend." I mean, I guess in a way it was a surprise, but anyway, the "friend" Chris was with was a slutty, not-nice girl named Kathy Connery (may you never

288

cross paths with her!), and she was the young lady having the affair with my then-boyfriend. They very well might still be having that affair, but it's not my concern, nor do I care. I needed evidence, and I sneaked into his backyard, climbed a grill, and took pictures of him and Kathy hooking up. And oh what pictures I snapped! I was so mad I was gonna plaster the pictures all over town, but luckily I have a best friend and a powerful, meditative conscience, so I didn't. I put the pictures in an envelope and asked you to hold on to the envelope so I wouldn't be tempted to do anything with the pictures. But life is just so different now, and I have no interest in the past. So . . . there we are. Caughtcha up! Sooo . . . however you can best destroy the "evidence," please do so. Thank you a ton and can't wait for Prom.

Your good friend,
Tara

JUNE 1992

Dearest Blooming Flower,

I wanted to tell you again that I had the most wonderful night at Prom with you. It will always be, for me, a snow-globe night I hold on to. And I will always get to open my wallet and look at our Prom picture.

No matter what hardships present themselves, I will forever be able to look at our Prom picture and know that I was the lucky one who lost her jean jacket. Because in return I got my jean jacket back, yes, but most importantly a lifelong friend.

You looked so handsome, and the paisley tux . . . so awesome! I'm just glad I wore my jean jacket over that dress. It got so cold at the after party.

What a fun, easy, and memorable night. I drew you a picture of us. I hope you like it. It's just a sketch of how I remember us that night. Laughing, enjoying, being happy.

I'm sorry again that I left the after party early. Justin really needed me. So much was going on at his house, so I'm glad I got to scoop him up and get him out of there. He and I will both be in colleges in Vermont next year, and I am glad they are different schools but I am also happy we won't be too far from each other. He's my best friend, whether we are "together" or not. I really hope you come visit me at Bennington!

I will always be here for you, Matt.

Thank you for being the best Prom date a girl could ask for, and I'm talking to my aunt and uncle today! They are the best, and I am almost positive they will find a spot for you at NYU Summer Theater School.

Biggest hug,

Stacey

Stacey,

I honestly had the best time at your Prom. How great was it when Stef and Diego were named Prom king and queen? I don't even know them, but they just seem like the nicest people. It was great to share the limo with all of them.

And no worries at all for leaving the after party. I'm just really happy you got to help Justin.

You better believe I will be visiting you in Vermont.

And I love your drawing. I am going to frame it.

I know you don't care about "stupid awards," but congratulations on getting Most Beautiful and Best Dressed. You are most beautiful, my friend, and hey, now the Stacey Simon jean jacket will live on forever in your yearbook!

Thanks for being you, and thank you SO, SO much for talking to your aunt and uncle for me! No matter the outcome I can't tell you how much I appreciate you offering that, Stacey. I still can't believe your aunt and uncle are the heads of admissions at NYU! So crazy.

Love,
Matt

P.S. I would love some wallets from Prom whenever . . .

To-est the Queen of South High,

No one deserves that title more than you, Stef. I loved our theme, "Hold On to the Nights," but man, it coulda also been "Oh, What a Night!" Because, you know what, Stef . . . oh what a night it was. For many a reason.

Is Kev Brandolini a magician, because that guy disappeared into thin air. Oh my god. He was awesome, though, and the important part is that everyone saw me with him and that we got pictures together! I could tell he wasn't wicked comfortable being there. I mean, he LOVED bein' with me, but the Prom itself felt wicked random for him. Hey, I don't blame him (things to do with South High have always felt wicked random for me, too).

Still can't get over "I've Had the Time of My Life" comin' on right when Christopher started talking to me. Thank you for grabbing me, Soup. Is there anything funnier than when you ran up like Baby and I held you up? If we could all be as little and petite as you! You gotta give Christopher a couple-a points for askin' me to dance at the end of the song, though. That was the most romantic thing he's ever done, and he's done so many! Just like your Diego!!

I can't believe *West Side Story* opens in 9 days and then we blink and high school ends.

Hey, we're leaving Most Talented, me, and Most Likely to Succeed, you. Oh, and you're our friggin' Prom queen! Not too shabby, You. Now don't go 'round gettin' wicked conceited 'cuz you're Prom queen and goin' to Northwestern AND dating a hot guy! I got my eye on you, Stefanie Wendy Campbell. Like you've always had yours on me, makin' sure I don't do anything to damage my reputation, I pinky promise to do the same for you. K?

And how thrilled are we for our dear Stacey that she got Most Beautiful and Best Dressed? I mean, hey . . . if those Superlatives didn't go to me or you, I know we are both wicked happy they at least stayed in the family and went to our other best friend.

I didn't tell you everything about the Christopher of it all. I left out the part where he offered me the ring back. Guess what I said? No thank you. (Besides, I think it turned my finger green.)

Love you to pieces,

Tara

To-est T-Murphs,

It is one thing that you were generous enough to dance with Chris. But, Tara . . . DO NOT TAKE THE RING BACK! Just be careful, Tar. You've come so far. Be careful and thoughtful here. And you know what? I don't need to know everything about the "Chris of it all." That's your business, and I have full faith you will do right by you.

I love you.

Soup

To my Tony,

We are so close to opening night, Matt. My final curtain at South High! Wow. As our fearless leader, I will do last looks on our *West Side* playbills in a couple of days. Tara Maureen Murphy, Matt Bloom, and Joy Rebecca Bernstein above the title, just like you wanted it.

My new perfume is Escape. I know, seems random me tellin' you that now, but you did ask back at the beginning of 1992 and I never did get around to tellin' you. I changed to Escape so I could leave 1991 in the past . . . so I could ESCAPE it. I needed the fragrance as a daily reminder to move forward, Matt. And move forward I have. So have you. So have we all.

It was awesome sharin' the dance floor with you, especially during "I've Had the Time of My Life." Stef and I are still dying over our dance routine. But there was that moment when you were twirlin' Stacey (her jean jacket looked so good over that skimpy yet sophisticated little dress of hers) and I caught your glance. And what a glance it was. Not sure I'll ever forget that Hungarian-slash-Russian-eyed glance of a Freshman. But time has a funny way of helpin' people forget, so one never does know.

If I was still someone who dwelled in what-could-have-beens I would be wondering what happened with the Matt and Tara that could've been more than friends. There was that moment, Matt . . . that moment in time when we were right there . . . But alas, now we are right here. In the now, not the then.

It's admittedly a little hard for me to see you and Joy kissing backstage, especially since I'm Maria, but I guess you belong together just the way maybe Christopher and I belong together.

I will always appreciate our talk outside at the after party. And thank you again for lending me your paisley tux jacket (pretty sure I told you this, but when a boy gives a girl his flannel or his jacket it usually means there is love in his heart). It was so cold and so windy you woulda thought we were in Chicago (Stef's soon-to-be new home). What's up with the nights bein' so friggin' cold and windy these days? It's June! Anyway . . . thanks for your jacket. It made one very frigid girl wicked warm—who knew your shoulders were THAT broad!

And Matt, I know you don't agree with me considering accepting Christopher back, but he was profusely apologetic, and I know him . . . he meant it. Am I gonna be with him again? Who knows? And if I do get back together with him, will it be forever? Not sure, I can't seem to find my crystal ball. Might I eventually end up with someone else who happens to be younger and multitalented? Perchance. I'm goin' to University end of August, Matt. That's just a fact. I know that, and I also know that right after graduation I am off to a cottage On Island. But that's it. That's all I know. The rest will reveal itself as it's meant to.

Hey, maybe we can find a few minutes to go to Camel Lot one last time before I skip this town forever. You still don't know why I call it that!

All my love,
Tara Maria

P.S. Sniff this note. When I'm long gone you can smell this college-ruled paper and . . . Escape . . .

Tara,

Hey, no problem about me lending you my tux jacket. It was really cold. And windy. When your hair got stuck to your lips I remembered you telling me about that time you were at the reservoir and that Timmy or Tommy guy pulled it off your lips. And that he then took you back to your house and dumped you. A real jerk, if you ask me. And that's all I could think about when you were telling me Chris asked you to get back together with him . . . Why would you do that to yourself? I know he told you that he made a mistake and that his life has been "miserable and lonely" ever since he broke up with you, but Tara . . . I don't know. I care about you and just want the best for you. Is he the best for you?

Anyway, yeah, I definitely want to go to Camel Lot with you so you'll finally tell me why you call it that!! This has been like *Waiting for Godot*!! But let's make sure to get over there before July 1st. That's when I ship off to New York. Oh my god, I just realized I haven't told you. This is so nuts. At Prom, Stacey and I got into this great conversation about life and the future and I told her how I already know I want to go to NYU no matter what. And she was like, "Why didn't you tell me that sooner?"

I was like, "Huh?" Anyway, long story wicked short . . . it turns out Stacey has an aunt and uncle who live in New York City . . . this place called the West Village on 12th Street and 8th Avenue, and they are this super artistic couple who met in acting school at NYU and fast-forward the VHS tape . . . they are now the heads of admissions at NY friggin' U! What are the chances? So, Stacey (being the thoughtful, great friend she is) called them and got me into their Summer Theater School (which is more a theater camp for high school kids, but still . . . it's NYU!!!). I guess she told them that she believes in my talent a lot, and she also sent them a tape of some of my original songs. I know you don't think too highly of NYU and turned them down, but I'm really excited. I am most excited to learn from serious acting professionals, but I am also excited just to live in a dorm downtown!! Even if it is just for six weeks!

So let's PLEASE go to Camel Lot before we both . . . Escape!

Matt "NYU SUMMER STUDENT" Bloom

To Zeke, Lloyd, Jimmy-Lee,
M . . . M . . . M . . . Matt!

I'm tellin' ya', end of Senior year really brings on the amne-
sia, Kid. I was like, "Tara . . . you know his dang name . . .
just think!" So I did just that, Eric. I put my pen down and
just thought. Made my head a blank canvas, and then just
like that . . . your name came right back to me. Don't ya just
hate when that happens?

I know this is wicked unfortunate, but I was goin' thru
my Month-At-A-Glance and realized there are just simply zero windows for me to take you to Camel Lot. I know,
bummer. And it's not like I'm gonna white-out any of my
graduation parties just to take you to Camel Lot. You think
I'd do that to my Senior friends? Just NOT attend their parties so I could take some random Freshman to MY SECRET
PLACE? 'Fraid not, Youngster. So as for Godot . . . keep
waitin'.

Your paisley tux jacket wasn't that warm, by the way. You
might wanna tell the woman at Bonardi's Tuxedo Shop that
'cuz knock knock . . . this is New England, not Southern
Florida! What's next? They gonna start pairin' their tuxedoes

with flip-flops?! This town can't even make their formalwear the right way. Jesus!

Hate to break it to ya, but Christopher Patrick Caparelli and I are officially back together! And when you see me in the hallways or at dress rehearsal, don't look at my finger unless you're fix'n to go blind! I've a polished claddagh ring on it, and oh man, does it bounce light, Matt! It's 14-karat gold, so yeah, when polished, it's wicked friggin' shiny!!

And one teensy-weensy favor, Matt . . . don't reference my stories back to me. "Uh, is it Timmy or Tommy?" Timmy. Timmy Garabino. You're remindin' me of Heather Gould. Years ago, in an effort for me to like her, she was like, "Hey, Tara. Remember when you worked at TCBY and that hot guy, Eli Spencer, always flirted with you and you always gave him free yogurt?" Uh, yeah, Heather. I remember. Wanna know how I remember? 'Cuz it happened TO ME, Lady! Not to you. Referencin' other people's stories back to them is somethin' I shoulda warned you about in 1991. It's trite, Matt.

Look at you goin' to NYU Summer Theater School! I'm always wary of places that happen to have a slot open super last minute, as it's usually a sign of vacancy, like if I was travelin' and in a jam, I would never stay at the hotel that happened to have an open room, ya know? Are you eating at the restaurant that HAS a table on a Saturday night? You probably are, but not this girl!

Is NYU Summer Theater School even ranked?

Ya know what, though, it'll be wicked good for you. You need the acting experience for sure.

Opening night can't come fast enough!!

Tara "Going to Actual College
Not Summer Camp College" Murphy

Dear Tara,

Are you okay? Your note seemed a bit abrasive. Not even one j to the k. I'll reread it, but it seemed like you're mad that I'm going to NYU even though I know that I must be wrong because you flat-out rejected their acceptance. Right? Did you know Stacey's aunt and uncle are the heads of admissions there? You must have known that, right?

Best,
Matt

Matt!

Yeah, of course I knew that one of MY closest friends' aunt and uncle were the goddamn heads of admissions at NYU! Have you met me?

Gotta run . . . I have some original songs to write.

Tara

Hello Stefanie,

Hi there. How are you? I hope all is wonderful in your multifaceted world. Everything is, as per usual, phenomenal in mine. Sooo close to gettin' outta here—not that I'm antsy, 'cuz I'm not. I'm wicked calm.

I have such a random question that literally just popped into my head out of the blue for no reason whatsoever, but did you know that our own Stacey Simon's aunt and uncle are the heads of admissions at NYU? I know . . . so random and who cares AT ALL, but did you know that?

Just get back to me on that as soon as you can, but there's no rush.

Love,
Tara

Tara,

They are? I had no idea. But we both know Stacey is so private. Such a small world, though. Of all places to be the heads of admissions . . . NYU? Wow! Are you sure they are? I mean, it does make sense, considering she told you years ago that she had an aunt and uncle who lived in the West Village and she even offered to hook you up with them if you ever moved to New York. Huh. I would say, "Are you okay?" but you got into THREE COLLEGES! So I know you are okay.

Love ya,
Stef

Stef,

Yeah, love ya too. Love ya too. And I'm sooooooo okay!! Almost no one gets into THREE COLLEGES in ONE DAY! Weird that Stacey never mentioned the NYU thingamajig, don't ya think? 'Cuz she, like, knew it was (at one time) my first choice, ya know? I mean, whatever . . . not that I care.

Oh, Christopher and I are a Supercouple again! And I did take the ring back, and I think before when I thought it turned my finger green it was just marker from my Month-At-A-Glance (you know how I color code everything in it), so it's definitely real gold. I was positive of that, but you know markers, Stef . . . they are prone to changin' the color of things. Even fingers (tee-hee, tee-hee).

I'm just gonna see if I can't meet up with Stace in F Hall between fifth and sixth periods just to calmly inquire about this whole silly, inconsequential NYU junk. It's all so trivial (pursuit . . I said it first), but hey . . . dear friends can ask dear friends about things, ya know? DYKWIM?

Hearts and Stars,
Tara

Tara,

Maybe don't even bother asking Stacey, right? Why even get into that? As you said yourself, "Who cares?" and it's "inconsequential." I say forget about it. Your opening night is right around the corner!! I can't wait to be front and center watching my superstar best friend in action!! So, yeah . . . my advice . . . just leave it alone.

I LOVE YOU!

Stef

Bloom!!!!

Are you okay??? I tried my best to keep Tara contained, but I guess I was focusing so much on her psycho-flailing arms I didn't even consider she could trip you!!! How the hell are her legs that long? Are they that long? I'm so much taller than her and I don't think I could've gotten my leg out that far. I mean, you weren't, like, a mile away, but you weren't like right near her either!! I guess 'cuz she's a cheerleader and kind of a dancer so she's flexible? But still, her leg just . . . well, I don't know how she got it out far enough to trip you!

What can I bring you for your face? I tried so hard, Bloom!! I hope you can still play Tony! What am I saying . . . you are Matt Bloom! The swelling could go down and will go down, I know it, Bloom!

Thank god Stacey Simon ran to get Mr. Flaherty! I guess it was lucky that she happened to be in F Hall at the same time, right?

Has Joy come to visit you in the nurse's office?

Seriously, anything you need from me, please, please, please tell me.

Pammy

Hey Pammy,

Believe me, I know how hard you tried. I can't believe all of that just happened. I still don't even know how any of it started, but I have some ideas. And trust me, I am going to find out!

Yeah, Joy is right here by my side. She says hi.

I think I can say for sure that neither you or I expected to see Tara swinging at Kathy Connery when we were just walking down F Hall. Jesus! I have to say, Pammy, I am so impressed with you. Blown away, actually. You just dropped your books and ran! You got right in between Tara and Kathy, and you were, like, pushing both of them away from each other! It was crazy, but you were incredible! You did everything you could do! I wish I had been able to help more, but by the time I got there to help you that friggin' leg came out of nowhere, and of course there had to be an open locker! I look like a Cabbage Patch Kid who just got the crap beat out of him. I don't know if I'll be able to play Tony, but you know me . . . I will do everything I can to get on that stage!!

You are awesome!! Never forget that!!

Matt

Blooming Flower,

Hi, my wonderful friend. How is that beautiful broken face of yours? More importantly . . . how is that beautiful heart of yours? I know violence like that does us both in, so I am really concerned about your heart.

What an amazingly brave and beautiful girl your friend Pammy is. Anyone would be lucky to call her friend. This is so unlike me, but please share with her that I think she is one great girl.

I'm just glad it all ended before it went further.

I am going to stop by your house tonight to bring you some chamomile tea bags. They really help with swollen eyes. As you know I've shed many tears, and these tea bags are my saving grace.

Love to you, my Blooming Flower.
Stacey

Bloom,

Kathy has cauliflower ear!!

Have you heard anything yet about how this whole thing started? And please tell Joy I say hi back!!

Pammy

Stacey,

First and foremost, thank you for checking in on me, and I would be so grateful if you came over tonight with those tea bags. Thank you.

That was so lucky that you were there and were able to get the principal. Did you see the whole thing go down? What even happened? Did Tara just start swinging at Kathy? I know you don't like to gossip so you don't have to tell me but you can if you want.

Love always,
Your Busted-Faced Blooming Flower

Blooming Flower,

You need to focus on getting better. You have a huge opening night coming up. That's all that matters.

It was all fairly quick and confusing. I was at my locker and Tara came up to me. She seemed really upset, but she was trying to, I don't know . . . it seemed as though she was trying to not be upset. I thought something was terribly wrong, so I asked her if she was okay. I went to give her a hug, and she kind of slapped at my arms. Which admittedly took my breath away. And then she said that you told her my aunt and uncle were the heads of admissions at NYU and that you agreed with her that I forced them to reject her from the University. Don't get upset. I know you never said that, my sweet friend. And I know I would never in a million years do anything like that. But Tara kept choosing not to believe me, and she started screaming in my face. That's when Kathy Connery showed up and just said, "Everything cool here?" That's when Tara sort of snapped. She forgot about me and turned all her rage on Kathy. Why? I have no idea. She just started calling her a "slut" and a "townie." Then she started swinging, and that is when you and the divine Pammy showed up.

But Matt, none of that matters. Truly. The only thing that matters is you healing.

See you tonight.

Big hug,
Stacey

Christopher!

Can you believe what that Kathy Connery did to me? Don't you wonder how any living human guy could hook up with her?? She is so gross and such a violent person! You haven't checked in on me, so I'm not sure if you're up to speed. Don't worry, Kathy at least had the decency to tell Mr. Flaherty that everything is settled, so there is no threat of suspension (for her, obviously) and everything will go on as scheduled, including and most importantly me as Maria in *West Side Story*. Thank god for my claddagh ring . . . it really came in handy when I needed to defend myself!!

Your Once-Again Girlfriend,
Tara

T,

I heard about everything that happened in F Hall. Real happy you are okay and not that I know Kathy all that well, but good on her for smoothing things over with Mr. Flaherty. So, it's all settled, right?

Love ya,
C.P.C.

Christopher,

Yes, it is all settled! There's nothin' to look at here, folks. Carry on, ya know what I mean? And yeah, wicked smart that Kathy Connery spoke the TRUTH to Mr. Flaherty. Girls like that are what bring towns down! Don't you agree? Not like you "know her all that well," but I'm sure you agree.

xoxo,

Tara

Stef,

Q even believe? Even Christopher is like, "That Kathy Connery is disgusting! What kinda girl starts fights?"

So, do you want the exact middle seat in the front row for *West Side Story*? Or, like, a few seats to either the left or right? Totally your call, but being a theater snob I truly think front row cuts off some of the show. Your best bet is third or fifth row CENTER! But you tell me, k?

Write back as soon as you can 'cuz tickets are sellin' wicked fast and I want my best friend to have the exact seat she wants.

Love you just as much as you love me,
Tara

Hey Tara,

It's pretty spectacular what 24 hours and a ton of chamomile tea bags can do. My face is just about back to normal. Sure, I still have a gash on my cheek from the locker I crashed into, but both Joy and Stacey think it looks cool and that having a really long, really big slice on my face will only add to the authenticity of my portrayal of Tony. So in some absurd way I want to thank you for TRIPPING ME.

I was walking down F Hall with Pam, and we saw you and Kathy throwing punches at each other. Knowing what I know (from you), I thought to help. Thank god Pam got in the middle of you two, because I bet Kathy would have more than cauliflower ear if she hadn't. But when I ran over to help, you saw me. I saw you see me, and you threw your friggin' leg out specifically to TRIP ME. Again, I have a great gash that will make my performance even stronger, but really? You TRIPPED ME? Why would you do that?

But most importantly . . . the thing I cannot get out of my head . . . the thing that is making me mad in a way I don't think I've ever been mad before is that you lied to Stacey. You lied to her and told her that I agreed with you that she used her family connections to make sure you got rejected from NYU!!! Are you kidding me?

First of all, Tara, I thought YOU rejected NYU! I thought YOU CHOSE NOT TO GO THERE! You know, because "No Quad," etc., etc., etc. You tried to pit me and Stacey against each other! Lying to her that I told you I AGREED with you that Stacey made sure you didn't get in there!! What planet are you living on?! Nice try trying to sabotage my friendship with Stacey, but it didn't work and NEVER WOULD!

I am so mad at you right now! After everything we've been through together you do this! To me! Why??

See ya around,

Matt

Dearest Matt,

Oh my GODDDD, you tripped? Babe, I am so sorry to hear that! The whole Kathy Connery thing was so chaotic, and then when that giant woman got involved I just lost my perspective. Like, totally gone! Matt, I would never trip anyone, let alone you! Are you sure Kathy or the Note-Readin' Candy Store Gossip didn't trip you, or maybe your sneaker sole caught a floor tile? You know these cheap, waxy floor tiles are prone to trippin' people up.

You got a gash on your face? Not the Keanu FACE!! You should sue the school. I bet that's exactly what your parents are thinkin' right this second! And good for them. This friggin' school deserves to be sued. Tell 'em to sue the entire town, while they're at it! But so glad you're healing. The notion of doing *West Side* without you (and with your understudy Ari Levy) makes me sick! Thank god that won't be happenin'!!

So you've fallen for the classic Stacey Simon spell, huh? Can't say I don't get it. There was a blip in time this year when I did, too. I know, I know. Me fallin' for anyone's trickery is shocking. Even to me it's shocking. But alas . . . spider-women like Stacey spin their silk so fast there's really no way to get away. She has her long brown hair (which she should cut, if you ask me . . . it's like, "Stacey, long hair is awesome and all, but that long? Seriously?") and her jean jacket and her "vulnerability" and her "everything is private and sacred" thing. She's what I call a Master Manipulator. You really gonna believe someone like her, Matt? Come off it . . . I know you better than that.

How excited are we for opening night? I'm gonna go shopping after school so I can get a great after-show outfit. Hey, this girl's gotta look amazin' when she meets and greets her fans. Ya know? Do you know what I mean?

To a Speedy Recovery . . .
Tara

P.S. Want me to bake you some of my famous gooey double-chocolate-chip cookies? Word is they make people feel better!

Tara,

No thanks. I don't want any cookies. I want you to tell me the truth. Admit that you tripped me intentionally and admit that you lied to Stacey. Admit this stuff to me, then maybe we can move on. Don't you think I deserve the truth from you, Tara?

Matt

Oh my GOD, Matt,

Listen, I am wicked sorry you've been injured. And that your injury is on your face . . . oh, Matt, how awful that must be. It makes me terribly sad for you, as I know how highly you regard that face of yours. I know that face of yours has been a calling card for you this year, as your entry into South High timed perfectly with Paula Abdul's release of the "Rush, Rush" video. But maybe it was time for the Matt Bloom/Keanu comparisons to end, ya know? You are such a unique kid, I for one wouldn't want you spendin' your entire high school experience livin' up to the expectations of a real movie star. But hey, I'm not gonna fib (not my style)—if I "got" tripped and got a gash on this face, well . . . I'd likely be gunnin' for someone to blame, too. So, do trust I feel your angst, Matt. As someone known for steppin' brilliantly and wicked authentically into other people's shoes (Connie Wong, Patty Simcox, Anne Frank, Maria, and the list goes on), I can absolutely step into yours and empathize with how you are feeling, Kiddo.

But as for your "admit it or else" note . . . sorry . . . but I just can't take your bait. Not sure what scheme you and Ms. Simon are cookin' up, but I've had my fill of chaos, Matt. The

329

people in this town have tried their darnedest to TRIP me up, but alas, I am college-bound and standin' tall (not as tall as your dear friend Pam . . . and don't think I don't see her tiny little pock-a-book . . . I see it. She can call herself Pammy and carry a mini pock-a-book all she wants, but those things can't conceal what these eyes see, k?).

You fell. In a hallway. At South High. And that plain sucks. I'll admit that, k, Matt? I'll gladly admit that trippin' in a South High hallway sucks. There . . . satisfied?

And while I'ven't a clue what hogwarsh Ms. Simon is throwin' your way, I can admit this: I don't care. Not interested in immature stuff like that anymore, Matt. Sorry to disappoint, but I've just evolved outta that. I know, bummer. Here you are just startin' to get excited by real-life drama and here I am literally so beyond it. Ahhh, life!

Now, back to our regularly scheduled program.

Opening night!!!! We are gonna give this town a story (a *West Side Story*) to remember!!

xoxo,
Tara

Um . . . Hello . . . Stef . . . You there?

WHICH SEAT WOULD YOU LIKE ME TO RESERVE FOR YOU?

TARA

Bloom—

I needed to tell you this, and I'm wicked sorry for being the one to tell you, especially because you're still healing, but I promised you I would never hurt you again and I don't want anyone else to, so I am just telling you, and whatever I can do to help you stop this I will.

There's a big rumor going around that you and Tara slept together outside of the Senior Prom after party.

You know how I work at Fanny Farmer Candy Shop? Duh, I know you know that, but okay, so . . . Kathy Connery works at the mall, too, at Coconuts, and she came into my shop—and oh man, is her cauliflower ear wicked bad—with Tricia Simms and Deena DeLuca, who are my friends or honestly as of now used to be my friends, and Kathy just started tellin' everyone that she saw you and Tara sleeping together, like, doing it together outside at this after-Prom party. She even said you did it on your paisley tuxedo jacket!!

I know you and Joy are basically back together or maybe you are together—I don't know because I'm only stage crew, it's not like I'm one of the leads or even in chorus, but I've known you my whole life and I just don't believe this rumor.

I know you probably don't care 'cuz you don't care what people think or say about you, and I know you don't need my help, but just if you do or anything . . .

Sorry again that I told you, but I just wanted you to know before this spreads around wicked fast, especially 'cuz *West Side* is opening tomorrow night, and after everything you've been through you deserve the best opening night ever!!

Pammy

Pammy,

Thank you so much for telling me. I appreciate it. And don't knock your role on stage crew . . . you are the eyes and ears of the whole production.

Glad you don't believe that pathetic rumor. Kathy Connery, huh? Never trust a woman (or women) scorned . . . but never mind about that.

By the way, I forgot to tell you that Stacey thinks you're incredible. How brave you were to break up that fight.

Okay . . . um . . . yes. Your help. Let me think about that, okay?

Thanks for everything,
Matt

Bloom,

Stacey Simon said that? Oh my GOD!! She's so pretty.

And seriously . . . let me know what I can do to help.

Pammy

Dear Pammy,

I took some time to think and you know what? I do actually
need your help. Can you swing by my house after rehearsal? I
know how to deal with this. I used to need my brother to help
me with shitty people like this, but man, I really grew up this
year! See you at my house, and bring your crew keys, okay?!

Thanks,
Bloom

Hey Tara,

So, are you sure you don't want to tell me the truth?

Matt

Hey Matt,

I told ya what I told ya, Matt. Look, if you wanna talk about
this further I can absolutely see if I can possibly carve out a
potential window to meet up with you. It's not lookin' wicked
likely (as my Month-At-A-Glance is chock-full . . . busy, busy,
busy), but I will for sure do you the solid of checkin'. Just don't
get your hopes up, k? And if and until we meet up, just chill
out, ya know? And hey, you, look at the bright side . . . it's
almost showtime!!!

Tara

P.S. How are you, by the way? I'm worried your trip-gash
did somethin' to your head 'cuz you're seemin' different, ya
know? Do you know what I mean? DYKWIM?

P.P.S. Free tip from me to you: Never falsely confess to
somethin' in a folded note. There are reading giants at science
desks 'round this neck-a-the-woods.

Tara,

Yeah, I think my "trip-gash" did do somethin' to my head. But that's a good thing. A very, veeery good thing. And no need to check your Month-At-A-Glance, k?

Matt Bloom

MATT!!!

What the HELL?! I slept at Christopher's last night, and when we went out to our cars this morning there were, like, a thousand copies of the pictures of him and Kathy all over his driveway and your street. They were everywhere, Matt!!

You told me you destroyed those photos!!

Christopher freaked out, Matt!! We were collecting them as fast as we could, but Chris was just faster than me, and it was like a friggin' popcorn trail that led right to your garbage cans. He freaked out!! And he was so confused and I was so confused and he was just like, "Where the hell did these come from?" He was getting so mad at me, Matt, and what was I supposed to do? We just got back together and everything has been goin' so good, so . . . I just had to tell him . . . I had to tell him that you must've seen Kathy's car there one night or somethin' and you must've, like, taken pictures of them.

I didn't know what else to say, Matt. This was all so unexpected! I thought you destroyed that envelope!!! Oh my god! Christopher is really pissed and I'm worried . . . what else could I have done in that moment?

Oh my god and it's opening night! How did this happen?

Tara

Dear Clara, I mean Sara, Mara, Farrah, Dara, Yara, Lara . . . shit . . . what on planet earth is your name? Maybe it starts with a *T*. Yeah, that's it. Is it Tina? Tanya? Tammy? Oh I just remembered . . . Tara.

What else could you have done in that moment? Oh, I don't friggin' know! Maybe tell the goddamned truth for once in your SENIOR life.

I can't wait until you get out of South High and out of this town!! Maybe then I can finally experience high school without feeling nauseous all the time. Maybe with you nowhere near this Mass Pike exit I can finally have the peaceful life I've so desperately wanted. You are a life-destroyer, Sara. T . . . T . . . rhymes with Sara, but it's . . . oh right . . . it's Tara. (My goodness, you have a wicked complicated name now, dontcha?!!)

You told Chris I must have taken the photos of him and that animal Kathy Connery?? Who are you? What are you? Because you can't be a human being. You just can't be. Will you stop at nothing to save your own ass? I can answer that:

YES. YOU WILL STOP AT NOTHING TO SAVE YOUR
OWN ASS.

To rewind the VHS tape, TARA, here's how shit went
down. I heard that Kathy Connery started a rumor that you
and I banged on my paisley tux jacket when we were outside the after-Prom party. So she must have been spying
on us, right? She must have eavesdropped on me lovingly
telling you to be careful and cautious with Chris this time
around. She must have heard me say to you, "Tara . . . I
know you want to accept his apology, but he still hasn't
admitted that he had an affair with Kathy." She took that
and was able to weave a rumor out of it. Just enough truth
for an evil person like that to build a flat-out rumor. My bet
is she wasn't gonna do anything this disgusting until YOU
got in a fight with her after YOU lied your friggin' face off
to MY GOOD FRIEND Stacey Simon! But once you gave
that Kathy Connery cauliflower ear, my guess is she started
thinking, "How can I get Tara back? How can I seek revenge
on Tara Maureen Murphy?" What does she care if she drags
me down with you? She doesn't know me. She doesn't give
a rat's ass if my reputation sinks to the bottom of the REZ
so long as YOURS goes down, too! And what the hell does
Kathy Connery have to lose? Chris got bored with her and
went back to you. Then you pretty much ruined her ear for
the rest of her life. Someone like that has NOTHING TO

LOSE. So, what does a spying eavesdropper who works at Coconuts and has zero to lose do? She goes into Fanny Farmer Candy Shop with a bunch of other derelicts and starts a blatant rumor that you and I were banging on my friggin' paisley tux jacket. What better way to get Chris all riled up again, huh? Thing Kathy Connery didn't count on was my SPY. Don't ever discount a lifelong friend who owes you one. That's a good tip for you goin' into your Freshman year, Tara. Oh, and when you get to college, don't go around trying to break friends up with lies, k? It's trite.

I'm almost a Sophomore, Tara Maureen, so guess what? I ain't takin' nobody's shit no more! Ya heard? I'm not the naive, sweet, innocent kid who walked into South High in September of 1991. Nah, I ain't that kid no more. I am a STAR! And guess what? I look like Keanu Motha-Fuckin' Reeves! I got long hair that I blow out of my face and all the girls love it! Especially Joy Rebecca Bernstein!! As someone said recently, "It's like havin' Julia Roberts and Keanu Reeves at our school!" Don't they know it! It's 1992, Tara. No one is spreading lies about me and getting away with it.

So I had some copies made. And you're right, I did say I would get rid of your stupid envelope, but I didn't because I forgot. I have a busy, busy, busy life too, and unlike you, I don't have a Month-At-A-Glance, so unfortunately I couldn't calendar "destroying Tara's pictures of Chris and Kathy hooking up." By the way, the days on your calendar can't get X'ed out fast enough!

I had the copies made, and man, was I mad. I was so mad I actually considered papering the town with those pictures. Ya know, the thing you were gonna do. But I took a breath, grabbed my Walkman, and went for a long walk, and guess where I ended up, Tara? At Camel Lot.

I sat there for a while, remembering every single moment of this entire year, and then I looked around and saw a sign. I walked up to it. It was a metal sign with a cute little camel on it. And under the cute little camel it said the word "Lot." Camel Lot.

I walked around the rest of the elementary school parking lot and saw a metal sign with an adorable penguin and the word "Lot" underneath that. Penguin Lot.

I saw a metal sign with a super sweet-looking elephant and guess what was underneath that elephant? The word "Lot."

Camel Lot is just the name of that part of the elementary school parking lot. And here I thought it was some interesting reference to the Kennedy family. The good news is that I do not need you to take me to Camel Lot so you can tell me why you named it that. 'Cuz guess what, Babe . . . you didn't name it that. It's just NAMED THAT!

When I figured all that out I just laughed. I laughed my ass off. I don't think I've ever laughed so hard in my life. My adrenaline slowed down and I thought, "You know what, Matt . . . you don't need to ruin anyone's life. You don't need to play dirty with dirty people. You are better than that." And I am. I am way better than that!

So I fast-forwarded the mix I was listening to and put on "Home Sweet Home" and I ran home. Fast. Fast, like someone in a movie who has figured it all out.

And by this time it was pretty dark out. I got the huge box of copies and I dumped them in my garbage cans. I thought that would be the end of things. And I was ready to just confront Kathy Connery gashed face to cauliflowered-ear face and tell her to stop spreading her bullshit. But you know what I forgot about, Tara? The winds at night. Like you said, it's been cold and windy at night, which is, in fact, so bizarre for June in New England. But Mother Nature has her way now, doesn't she? I guess she had a little meditative think, too, and she chose to blow my garbage cans down and scatter thousands of copies all over my street and Chris's driveway. Who woulda thunk?

Good luck tonight, Tara! It is, in fact, your last opening night.

And best of luck to you in all your future endeavors. K? Ya know? Do you know what I mean? DYKWIM?

Matt Bloom 1992

FOLDED NOTES FROM HIGH SCHOOL

P.S. Oh my god, I almost forgot to tell you. Before I wrote this note I told Chris everything. He now knows that you are the one who sneaked into his backyard, climbed a grill, and snapped those photos. He's wicked pissed. So . . . just a heads-up!!!!!!

Hiiiii Matt!!!

Oh my god, opening night was so good!! You were amazin', and I especially loved the last-minute twist you put on Tony. I've never even considered him bein' played like he hates Maria, but that was definitely unique and clever. Not that I'd expect anything less from someone of your caliber!

Did you like my after-show outfit? I'm gonna assume you loved it even though you didn't say anything about it or anything at all. But we were both swarmed with people after the show, so I know there wasn't much time to chitchat. I was like, "Tara, go find Matt to talk about how awesome the show was!" But there were just too many folks to give time to, ya know?

So odd that both Stef and Christopher didn't show up. I'm sure they're coming tonight. Or maybe they will just wait for closing night, as everyone knows that's the best performance of the run. And the energy of closing night (especially closing night of the Spring Musical, especially it being MY final show at South High) is gonna be off the charts!!

Your note to me was so sweet. I'm not bein' condescending 'cuz I'm sure you thought it was tough-guy-ish, but I thought it was so sweet. Just how you've grown up a bit. That note was really a sign of you attempting to find your voice, and Matt . . . I definitely think you are more than ready to be a Sophomore.

And look at you bein' a private investigator and crackin' the case of Camel Lot. Sometimes (and remember this as you head into your Sophomore year) the answer to what you think is impossible to figure out is often actually right in front of your nose, hidin' in plain sight.

After closing night wanna get in my Wagoneer and head over to Camel Lot one last time? Even though you know why it's called that I might just have another surprise for you. It's nothin' major, just a show gift of sorts. So? What say you, Young-but-More-Mature Man?

And by the way, both Joy and Stacey were spot-on, Matt. The cut on your face does add a certain somethin'. Who woulda thunk it?

Be good, You,
Tara Maureen Murphy

P.S. Was that a prop ring on Joy's finger? It looked like a claddagh ring, but it wasn't, was it? Not that I care.

The South High correspondence ends there. But a recently uncovered envelope postmarked September of 1992 from Tara Maureen Murphy at Boston College suggests there's more to the story than we may ever know.

The White House
1992

29 USA

BOSTON
29 SEP
1992

Matt Bloom
14 Calypso Lane
Framingham MA 01701

Tara Maureen Murphey
90 Hayden Hall, Boston College
1633 N Boylston Street
Boston, MA 01812

Acknowledgments

So grateful to Sara Crowe at Pippin Properties you are an agent like no other and you reignited my faith at every turn. I am "heartened" that I get to do all of this with you.

Where my New York State Thruway Rest-Stop crew at? Jordan Galland, what a great call to get a coffee en route to the Catskills. Your friendship, the Gramercy walk/talk, your generosity—without you there is no this. Jessica K. Almon— the dream-maker, my creative partner. Thank you for giving me the shot. I debut because of you. Thank you for taking the torch, Marissa Grossman—no one else I would rather cross the finish line with. Katherine Quinn—you were the missing piece to the puzzle—thank you for joining our team. And to the guy who made me feel like Charlie Bucket—Ben Schrank, thank you for everything. To everyone at Razorbill and Penguin, this has been a dream come true!

David Krintzman—you have been by my side and had my back from the very beginning. Your friendship, counsel and belief in me has meant more than you know. And to everyone at Morris Yorn, especially Ashley Nissenberg and Kristi Eddington—thank you for everything.

Michelle (Meesh) Pollack—for carrying my dream when I couldn't and reminding me always it was possible—I pull up my bootstraps because of you (and then place m'boots neatly where they belong. . . because of you.)

My gorgeousess—Evvy Delilah and River Gracie—you are the constellation I looked for my entire life. "When you're standing next to me somewhere else I feel like I'm at home!"

David Boren—I pitch to you and send you pages because if my big brother likes it and laughs, I feel like I can do anything.

Lisa, Ben, Jonah and Eli Boren—you have given me the greatest gift in the world—a safe stage to try out all of my material... EVEN!

And to my Mom(my) and Dad—Here we are.

Endless thanks for your check-ins, words of wisdom, early eyes, love and support throughout this journey—David Castagnetti, Joy Cohen, Josh Stelzer, Chloe Jo Davis, Phil Eisen, Ginger Sherak, Mike, Po, Sam and Zach Boren, Kevin Simms, Jennifer Posner, Rebecca Budig, Justin Warfield, Vicki Davis, Paul Ellis, Jess Pollack, Aaron Hitchcock, Brett and Libby Hansen, Jessica Golden, Jonathan Texera, Kathy Rivkin, Emily Alexander, Lori Price, Matt Silverberg, Melissa Steinitz, Jordana Arkin, Adam Shapiro, Sabrina Eisenstadt, Justin Shilton, Joanne and Bill Pollack, Estee Stanley, Sharon Lee, Austin Winsberg, Erica Baritz, Jonas Vail, Stacey Price, Justin Leigh, Meredith Salenger, Gwynne Pine.

Matt Boren has written over eighty-five episodes of television for *Melissa and Joey*, *See Dad Run*, and *Sofia the First*, among others. Boren has acted in many projects in both film and television, including nine seasons as Stuart on *How I Met Your Mother*. He lives in Los Angeles, California, with his family. *Folded Notes from High School* is his first novel. Follow him on Twitter @Borentown.

To Kerry Foster and Elizabeth Dutton for knowing.

Forever gratitude to Kelly Ripa—you made this vision board complete.

To every dreamer, it is possible. To every kid who is different, thinks you're different, is told you're different—you're in good company. Harness positively that which makes you unique, create new paths for those behind you and know you are not alone. . . no one is.